She was

"I'm not sure how much longer I can keep you safe from me," Grant murmured. "I want you."

The need between them vibrated so intensely, Mattie could almost hear it, like a wire pulled taut and about to be struck. Maybe safe wasn't what she wanted. Maybe she wanted Grant Whittaker.

She took a step forward, he took a step back. "Stay," she whispered, putting a hand on his solid chest, feeling his warmth, his heartbeat.

He held her off. "Mattie, if I stay now, we're going to make love."

She gave him a slow sensual smile, then took his hand and drew him into the room. "Didn't you once threaten to make love to me on this couch..." Bracing one leg on the cushion, she started to unbutton his shirt and whispered, "Many times?"

"I've always dreamed of being a gourmet cook," confides talented author **Carolyn Andrews**. "So writing *The Marriage Curse* gave me a chance to explore one of my secret fantasies. Even more fun was being able to revisit the Farrell family from my very first Temptation novel, *C.J.'s Defense*." Carolyn lives in Syracuse, NY, where she spends her days trying to write enough books to keep her editor happy.

Books by Carolyn Andrews

THE MARRIAGE CURSE
Carolyn Andrews

Harlequin Books

TORONTO • NEW YORK • LONDON
AMSTERDAM • PARIS • SYDNEY • HAMBURG
STOCKHOLM • ATHENS • TOKYO • MILAN
MADRID • WARSAW • BUDAPEST • AUCKLAND

To my sons,
Kevin, Brian & Brendan.
You're the best!

ISBN 0-373-25681-7

THE MARRIAGE CURSE

SHE WAS LATE. Mattie Farrell pulled into the parking lot of George's Diner, crawled across the gearshift of her red Toyota, and climbed out the passenger door. The driver's side was tied shut with electrical tape. Just until she had the money to fix the latch. And that would be right after she replaced the spare tire. Mattie gave it an apprehensive look as she circled the front of the car. Not that it bore much resemblance to a real tire. It looked more like a cross between an inner tube and a doughnut. Nor was it meant for long-distance driving. The man who had pulled over to help change her flat had emphasized that quite strongly. Thank heavens, it had gotten her to Barclayville.

She could not afford to miss this appointment with Grant Whittaker. Her plans for expanding her new restaurant depended on his cooperation. If only she knew more about him. Reaching through the open window of her car, she grabbed her briefcase from the back seat. She'd never met the mystery man of Barclayville. The original lease on her restaurant had been handled by Grant's friend George Schuler.

Mattie glanced at her watch as she hurried toward the long, low-slung building that housed Barclayville's only diner. It was one-thirty. She was a half hour late. She hated to have her schedule thrown off by something she couldn't control. She'd allowed an hour for this meeting. Half of it was already gone. And the Millers, her seven o'clock reservation, wanted a *bombe au chocolat* for dessert tonight.

At the foot of the steps, she paused. *Confidence*, she reminded herself. That was how she'd gotten the lease on Whittaker House in the first place. Initially, George Schuler had been skeptical about her desire to open a gourmet restaurant in such a small town. He claimed it was her confidence that finally persuaded him to get his old friend Grant to sign on the dotted line. Now, a year later, Whittaker House was operating at a nice profit. It was time to expand.

Switching her briefcase to her other hand, Mattie wiped her palm on her jeans. She'd be feeling a lot more confident if she were dealing with George today. But fate in the form of a bad fall had put the seventy-five-year-old man temporarily in a nursing home. And after an absence of eighteen years, Grant Whittaker had returned to Barclayville to run the diner until George recovered from hip surgery.

Mattie drew in a deep breath and let it out, hoping to still the butterflies in her stomach. Silly to be so nervous. After all, Mr. Whittaker had gone along with George on the first lease. Surely he wouldn't give her a problem about expanding into the old Barclay mansion, not when she was offering him an opportunity to make a profit on some real estate that had stood vacant for almost fifty years.

Squaring her shoulders, Mattie climbed the steps to the diner. Her own motivations went a lot deeper than money. Running a successful country inn was her dream. Convincing Grant Whittaker to cooperate would give her the chance to prove to herself and her family that she could do it. She'd failed miserably in her first attempt. Even now, it hurt to think about how her partner, Mark Brenner, had forced her to sell her shares of the inn they'd run together in Maryland. Well, she'd never make the mistake of going into a partnership again. This time, she wasn't depending on anyone else to help her achieve her dream, not even her family. And she wasn't going to fail.

Mattie tried the door and found it locked. Frowning, she rapped on the glass. When there was no response, she began to tap her foot. Then, shading her eyes, she peered inside. Dust motes swirled in the sun that streamed through the window over the grill and splashed across a long, narrow counter. The place was empty! During the week, the diner was only open for breakfast. That was why Grant had set the appointment for one o'clock. Surely he couldn't have thought she'd stand him up. A truck racing past on the highway whipped up the still air. Above the scent of sun-heated tar and new-mown grass, Mattie smelled something fresh-baked. *The kitchen.* She hurried toward the back of the building.

Turning the corner, she found her path blocked by a black motorcycle. It was a huge two-seater with a windshield and a storage compartment. There was even a luggage rack over the rear fender. Grant Whittaker's? Mattie stared at it curiously. All she knew about him was that he taught classes at Cornell in the hotel management school when he wasn't traveling around the country doing consulting work.

Did he make his trips on a motorcycle? Mattie kept her gaze on the bike as she detoured around it. She had pictured Mr. Whittaker as a contemporary of George Schuler's, an elderly, debonair professor type with graying hair and a pipe. The image didn't fit the big black bike.

A muffled bark drew her attention to a path that led away from the back of the diner. Though she couldn't see a dog, Mattie spotted the man immediately. He was about fifty yards away, all but hidden in the folds of a hammock that hung from two elm trees.

Nice work if you can get it, she thought as she fixed a polite smile on her face and walked toward him. Obviously he had it made in the shade. And it looked cool and inviting, too. Close by, she could hear the sound of water rushing over rocks. Mattie reached behind to unstick her shirt from her back and tried not to think of her own day, which had started at five a.m. and promised to go on forever.

He was asleep. Her gaze rested briefly on his chest; it was rising and falling in a steady rhythm. It was also bare. In fact, the only interruption in the expanse of tanned skin stretched taut over bones and muscle was a very brief pair of faded cutoffs. With an effort, Mattie forced her gaze upward to his face, which was half-hidden by a baseball cap. The man she was looking at was in his thirties, at least forty years younger than George Schuler. His hair was thick and the rich, tawny color of a lion's mane without a hint of gray. It curled out from under the cap, and there was more sprinkled liberally over his chest, his arms and down the length of his strong legs. With no effort at all, Mattie could imagine how his hair would feel beneath her hands. Soft, with a silky, springy texture. She was stepping forward, reaching out with one hand just as the man let out a long sigh and shifted slightly.

Mattie took a quick step back. She'd wanted to touch him. If he hadn't sighed just then, she would have. What had she been thinking? Her stomach growled, and she pressed a hand to it. That was her problem. She was hungry. Her stomach growled again as if in confirmation of her theory.

GRANT WHITTAKER let out a very long sigh and shifted in the hammock. He'd been back in Barclayville less than a week, and already the need to escape was building. More than anything, he wanted to hop on his motorcycle and hit the open road. But he couldn't do that. The one person in the world who had never let him down was George Schuler. Not only had George taken him in and raised Grant from the time he was ten, the old man had also instilled in him a love of learning that had eventually won him a scholarship to college and a job at Cornell University.

No, running away was not an option, so he'd settled for a nap. Perhaps if he stayed in the hammock long enough, the whole depressing prospect of spending the summer in his hometown would turn out to be a dream. Hopefully a pleasant one, since his earliest years here had been more like a nightmare.

At eighteen, he'd left the dust of Barclayville behind forever, he'd thought. Of course, he'd been young, college-bound and full of himself, so it had temporarily slipped his mind that life didn't hand out *forevers*. Even though it was a lesson he'd learned the hard way at the age of five when his mother had been killed in a car accident. And then relearned at ten when his father had deserted him. And just in case he'd forgotten that nothing lasts forever, the breakup of his marriage five years ago and the ongoing custody battle for his son had reminded him once again.

So here he was, back home in Barclayville. No, not home, Grant reminded himself. As soon as George recovered from surgery, he'd take off like a shot. With a faint frown, he shifted again and tried to clear his mind. Nearby, he could hear the sound of water rushing over rocks. Soothing. Upstate New York wasn't far from the Catskills where Rip Van Winkle had taken his twenty-year nap. Maybe the strange little men with their game of ninepins would find him and cast their magic spell. Not that he wanted to sleep two decades. Just the summer would do.

And then he heard it. A rumble. Too soft for thunder. Or bowling balls. It sounded more like a growl. In one smooth movement, Grant shoved off his baseball cap, swung his legs over the side of the hammock, and sat up.

The first thing he noticed about her was her eyes. They were deep blue, almost violet. Perhaps an illusion created by contact lenses. But everything else looked authentic. His gaze moved slowly over her. There were too many shades of red and gold in her hair for the color to have come out of a bottle. He liked the way she wore it, pulled back from her face and fashioned into an intricate braid by some feminine bit of magic. A few curls had pulled loose to frame her face. Very tempting. The June sun was hot, but the lady managed to look neat and cool in tapered white jeans and a white shirt with a red pouch strapped around her waist. Her shoes were red, too, with platform soles and thin, crossed straps. Very interesting. If this was a dream, it had definite possibilities. Grant shot her a smile.

"I'm looking for Grant Whittaker," she said.

His smile widened. "You've come to the right place."

"You're Mr. Whittaker." It wasn't a question. Suddenly, Mattie was certain that the man sitting in front of her was the man who held her future in his hands. He certainly went with the motorcycle better than the aging professor she'd pictured.

"In the flesh. Call me Grant."

Definitely in the flesh, Mattie thought as her eyes dropped to the nicely defined muscles in his shoulders, and then to his chest. Her stomach growled again. Quickly, she fished in her red pouch for a roll of antacids. She pulled out candy instead.

"What can I do for you?" Grant asked.

"Look, I'm sorry I'm late for our appointment." Popping the candy into her mouth, she handed him a business card. "I had a flat tire." She glanced at her watch and noticed that ten more minutes had ticked inexorably away since she had pulled into the parking lot. Mattie thought of the *bombe au chocolat*. She'd just have to stall the Millers for a while with a complimentary appetizer. When she looked back at Grant, she saw him glance up from her card to study her through narrowed eyes.

"Ms. M. Farrell. You *can't* be the lady who runs the gourmet restaurant in my old ancestral home."

He certainly didn't look happy about it. *Confidence*, Mattie reminded herself once more as she beamed a smile at him. "Yes. In the flesh, so to speak."

"I thought you'd be older."

It sounded like an accusation. A little puzzled, Mattie said, "I thought you'd be older, too. Since you're a friend of George's—" Once more, she was interrupted by her stomach.

"C'mon." Grant rose, and Mattie had a brief vivid impression of height before he took her arm and began to urge her back up the path to the diner. "You can eat something while we discuss business."

Mattie was about to protest, when a very large, very dirty dog came loping up the path. Before she could get out of its way, the animal leaped up to plant two muddy feet on her shirt and a sloppy kiss on her mouth.

"Down, Hannibal." Grant gave the command as she fell back against him. "Are you all right?"

Mattie didn't reply at once. His chest felt like a rock at her back. She couldn't help noticing. Just as she couldn't help noticing that she was a little breathless, as if she'd just raced to the top of a very steep hill. And she couldn't seem to feel her knees, especially after he turned her in his arms.

"Are you all right?" he asked again.

"Fine." Her voice sounded weak. Perhaps because it was hard to hear over the pounding of her heart. Clearing her throat, she tried again. "I'm fine. Really."

"Sorry," he said. But he didn't release her. They were face-to-face. This close he could see the darker, almost purple flecks in her eyes. And he caught her scent for the first time. It reminded him of vanilla. His gaze dropped to her mouth, and lingered. Just as he was beginning to wonder how she would taste, she stepped back.

The dog barked, but this time Grant caught hold of its collar before it leaped up to try for another kiss. "Shame on you, Hannibal."

Once the animal was sitting, thumping its tail, Grant turned his attention back to Mattie. He watched her lean down to acquaint herself with the dog and waited for his system to level. But it didn't right away. All he had to do was look at her, and he could recall exactly how she'd felt in his arms. More slender than she looked, more fragile, too. For a moment, he'd wanted to kiss her. He still wanted to.

With a slight frown, he shifted his gaze to her hands as she stroked Hannibal. She wore a ring, a twist of gold with a small stone that caught the light. On her right hand, not her left.

Grant's frown deepened as he tried to remember everything that George had told him about the woman who was leasing Whittaker House. Not much except for the decades of experience she'd had in the restaurant business. Decades? He watched her rise in one fluid movement. Not unless she'd been some kind of child-prodigy chef hatched in an oven.

"Look, Mr. Whittaker—"

"Grant." It was only as she turned that Grant saw the muddy paw prints. "Your shirt's ruined. I'll replace it."

"It's just dirt." The dog barked again as he maneuvered his head under her hand. "See. Now he's apologizing. Is he yours?"

"He pretends to belong to anyone who feeds him. And speaking of food, you're in luck. Today's special is blueberry buckle, and if you share with Hannibal, he's yours." Grant took her arm and hurried her down the path.

Inside, the diner was spotless. The faint scent of pine cleaner lingered in the air, and even the chrome that edged the counter gleamed. Mattie climbed up on a stool, settled her briefcase beside her, and opened it.

"Pleasure before business," Grant said as he placed ice coffee and a slice of blueberry buckle in front of her. Mattie stared at the cake. "It's blue."

"That's why they call them blueberries."

"But the whole cake is blue," Mattie said.

Grant winked at her and said in a confidential tone, "This is a diner, not a fancy gourmet restaurant. We don't have the time to worry a lot about appearance or presentation. The berries were so big and ripe, they bled into the batter a little. Taste it."

Stalling, Mattie took a sip of ice coffee. The square of cake really did look awful. Almost purple, like a bruise. "Good food should appeal to all the senses," she said, stalling.

"We're very informal here. Go ahead, sniff it first, if you like."

He was laughing at her. She could hear it in his voice, see it in the way his eyes crinkled at the corners. She was tempted to join him, but first she drew in a deep breath. To her surprise, the cake smelled better than it looked. Much better.

Hannibal let out a howl, and Grant tossed him a slice. Mattie watched it arc through the air. The dog caught it, swallowed it whole and settled into a mound in front of the door.

"See? Hannibal likes it, and if we're going to discuss business, it will go a lot faster if we don't have to do it over the noise your stomach's been making."

Resigned, Mattie shoved a forkful of blue cake into her mouth. Suddenly, a combination of flavors exploded on her tongue. The tartness of the berries sharply contrasted with the sweetness of the cake. Not too sweet, though. More nutty. And then there was the tang of the berries that lingered even after she swallowed. She took another bite. "Delicious." She took a third mouthful. When the plate was free of the last crumb, she looked up to find Grant grinning at her.

"There's got to be a way to make it look better," she said.

"Probably. But in a diner, we believe that the bottom line is taste."

"In a fancy gourmet restaurant, we believe that appearance and presentation improve taste."

Grant's gaze moved slowly to her lips and lingered there before his eyes met and held hers. "We could conduct a little experiment, and test your theory, if you'd like."

Mattie felt the shiver of response right down to her toes. Fighting it, she met his killer smile with one of her own. "Give me the recipe, and let me play around with it."

His laugh was so quick and infectious that she found herself wanting to join him.

"Nice try. But I'm sworn to secrecy. You'll have to ask George for it."

"How is George?" she asked.

"Complaining to the doctors that he can't run yet and flirting outrageously with all the nurses." Grant leaned back against the cold grill to study Mattie for a moment. "You know, the more I think about it, the more convinced I am that George deliberately misled me about your age to get me to sign your lease. He told me you'd had decades of experience in the restaurant business, that you'd run a successful country inn in Maryland."

"He didn't lie. I started cooking in my mother's restaurant in Syracuse right after my father was killed. My brother and sister, too. We all helped. I was ten, so that's almost twenty years ago, and I did own an inn in Maryland for a year."

"And you left Maryland for Barclayville?"

Mattie concentrated on relaxing her hands the moment she realized how tightly clasped they were. "I had problems with my partner. Not financial ones. The inn was—still is—successful. Why is my age a problem?"

"Because if you were older, it wouldn't matter so much. Hell, George knew my feelings." Grant paused to run a hand through his hair. How could he explain? "He even had me thinking that he was sweet on you." The baffled look on her face told him that he wasn't making sense. "I'd better start at the beginning. I inherited Whittaker House and the old mansion on the hill behind it when I was seventeen. I swore then that they'd remain empty for as long as I owned them."

"Why?" Mattie asked.

"Because I figured they'd already ruined enough lives."

"How?"

"Let's just say that there's a long history of bad luck associated with both houses. And once they became my responsibility, I wanted to put a stop to it."

"So, if I were George's age, I wouldn't have much time left to ruin. Is that what you were thinking?" she asked as she reached for her drink.

"Yes. I guess that was my reasoning. It's not as though I've had to turn a lot of people down. Whittaker House has been vacant for the past twenty-five years." He took her plate and put it in the sink. "Everyone blames it on the ghost."

Mattie choked on her ice coffee. "Ghost?" A wave of coughing overtook her.

Grant leaned across the counter to pat her on the back. "I know it sounds funny." He could hardly blame her for laughing. He felt silly even talking about it. As soon as she could manage a steady breath, Grant continued, "Personally, I think it's a crock. But the whole town believes that my great-aunt haunts Whittaker House."

"You don't believe that?"

"I always figured no self-respecting ghost would hang around this town. And for that matter why would you?

You're young. You have your whole life ahead of you. I know you came here today to make a change in the lease agreement. But I'd be willing to release you from it entirely. In fact, I'd feel a lot better if I could do that. The best advice I can give you is to get out of Barclayville."

Get out of Barclayville. Mattie stared at him. It sounded like a line from a vintage western. She would have laughed, but there was no mistaking the intensity in his voice, in his body. She could almost feel it, radiating across the counter at her. She pressed a hand to her stomach. The tightness, the heat, it couldn't possibly be hunger she was feeling this time.

Then a thought suddenly occurred to her. In all her careful preparation for this meeting, it was the one possibility that she had not considered. And she should have. Hadn't Mark Brenner forced her out of their inn once he'd used her to establish its success? Was Grant Whittaker hoping to do the same thing by piggybacking on the reputation of Whittaker House? Blue cake or not, he had plenty of background in managing hotels and inns. Mattie looked at him intently. "Do you have some plan to open your own restaurant here? Is that why you're so anxious to get rid of me?"

Grant shook his head impatiently. "No. As soon as George recovers from surgery, I'm out of here. Look." Grant paced down the length of the counter, then turned to face her. "Barclayville just isn't a good place to settle down in."

Mattie smiled in relief. "You don't have to worry about that. I'm not thinking of living here, just running a successful business. And the restaurant is doing very well. Especially when you consider that it's only open Thursday through Sunday." She pulled two documents out of her briefcase and placed them side by side in front of him. "In fact, business is so good that I want to expand."

"Expand? How?"

"The old mansion you own on the hill behind Whittaker House. I want to fix it up. A little paint, some wallpaper, add a few bathrooms and offer overnight accommodations. In addition to guests, I think that I can attract small businesses and some of the nearby college faculties for seminars, retreats, miniconferences." She pointed to a folder. "This contains a complete two-year business plan with some very conservative profit projections." Then she ran her finger down the first page of the lease. "These terms are the same as those for Whittaker House. I still have the option to buy within three years. There's just one difference." She flipped to the last page. "Since there is some risk involved, I'm giving you a fifteen percent share of the profits." She offered him a pen.

Grant ignored it. "You can't be serious. Have you talked to anyone in town about this?"

Mattie nodded, still holding out the pen. "I've mentioned it to the Clemson sisters. George was kind enough to send them to help me out at Whittaker House."

"And they encouraged you? They didn't mention the curse?"

Encouraged wasn't the word Mattie would have chosen to describe the Clemson sisters' reaction to her plans. Quickly she latched on to the word *curse*. "What curse?"

"On the Whittakers and the Barclays and on anyone who has ever had anything to do with the place, even servants, deliverymen, you name it. The Whittaker Curse has pretty much driven anyone under the age of seventy out of Barclayville."

Mattie watched him pace behind the counter. A curse? She reached for her ice coffee and then thought better of it. Maybe the caffeine was what was making her feel like Alice In Wonderland falling headfirst down the rabbit hole. When Grant stopped in front of her, she said, "You don't believe in the ghost, but you believe in a curse."

He leaned toward her. "Don't you think I feel ridiculous just talking about it? But I believe in facts. And there are plenty to support the existence of the Whittaker Curse."

He was close. This close his eyes were the color of mist. Mists were dangerous. They made her think of Brigadoon and hundred-year enchantments. And curses? Very carefully, Mattie set down the pen and inched backward on her stool. "What exactly are they blaming on your great-aunt?"

"Unhappy marriages." Grant stifled the urge to swear. Put into words, the curse always sounded so . . . lame. He hastened to explain further. "Ever since my great-aunt jilted Peter Barclay, no one associated with the Barclay mansion has been able to stay married. They get divorced," he added.

"That's it?" Mattie had to try hard to keep her expression serious. She didn't dare laugh, or even smile. He was so obviously concerned. She cleared her throat. "You must know that this marriage curse isn't limited to the residents of Barclayville. More than half the marriages in the country end in divorce." Trying to exude confidence, Mattie picked up the pen and offered it to Grant again. "I'm willing to risk it."

"No. I can't do anything about your lease on Whittaker House, but I won't help you expand into the Barclay mansion."

Mattie beamed her best smile at him. "How about if I put in writing that I won't get married? I'm going to be much too busy. And I know from experience not to mix business with personal relationships."

"I can see you think this is a joke. Believe me, I know what it sounds like put into words, but I assure you—"

The phone rang. Grant grabbed the receiver on the wall near the grill. "Joel. How was San Diego?"

The friendly tone of his voice kept Mattie's attention on him. He was a complicated man. Beneath that surface layer of happy-go-lucky charm, Grant Whittaker had a more serious side. And she was sure he meant well. But sometimes, well-meaning people could be very frustrating. She thought of her family. They meant well, too, especially her older brother, Roarke. But ever since she'd returned from Maryland, he'd hovered around her like a guardian angel. And when the district attorney played protector, it could be embarrassing. When he ran a background check on one of her dates, she'd known opening her restaurant in Barclayville had been the right decision.

In a way, Grant reminded her of Roarke. She'd have bet the *bombe au chocolat* that was going to be *very* late arriving at the Millers' table tonight that he wasn't opposed to her expansion plans for any other reason than his desire to protect her. From a so-called curse! Well, she'd learned long ago that the best defense against an overprotective brother was to give him a wide berth. She'd handle Grant Whittaker the same way, as soon as she got him to sign the lease. Her train of thought was interrupted when Grant's tone changed.

"Yeah, your secretary gave me the message." Grant paced as far as the phone cord would allow. "The lack of excitement that you hear in my voice is directly related to my knowledge of my ex-wife. If Lisa is willing to give up custody of our son, there's a catch. I've been waiting for you to interpret the fine print before I open the champagne." Grant paused for a moment as he glanced at his watch. "Okay. I'll be in your office by four."

Mattie felt her stomach sink. Her gaze dropped to the two documents in front of her. The lease agreement on the Barclay mansion was two pages long. The language was precise, objective. It would take a literate person about five minutes to read through it. How long would it take to read a custody agreement? she wondered. How would a parent get through it, knowing that it affected the future of a child?

And she had made light of the curse. When she looked at Grant, he was staring through the plate-glass window of the diner. Though he was standing perfectly still, she could sense his tension, his restlessness. It was the way she felt whenever her temper threatened to break loose.

"Mr. Whittaker," she said as she slid from the stool.

"Grant." The response was automatic, but his eyes never left the parking lot.

"Why don't I leave the papers? You can look them over later." Mattie made it to the door only to find her exit blocked by a mound of canine fur. Stepping around Hannibal, she tried to open the door. Neither it nor the dog budged.

"The way to Hannibal's heart is always through his stomach."

Mattie turned to find Grant waving a piece of blueberry buckle. When he tossed it a few yards, the dog rose and lunged forward in pursuit. Grant grinned at Mattie. "A taste good enough to move mountains. How can you argue with that?"

"Who knows what it might move if it looked better?" she said as she opened the door. But she was relieved to see that the faraway look had disappeared from his eyes. "And speaking of tastes, I have a few of my own to create for dinner tonight. I'll leave the papers until we can talk again."

Grant watched her hurry down the steps. It was on the tip of his tongue to tell her that she could talk all she wanted, she'd never convince him to change his mind about leasing the Barclay mansion. But then he became distracted by how she walked in that quick fluid way. In spite of the height of her platform shoes. Lovely.

He followed her to the car. "If we're going to talk again, we should be on a first-name basis. You haven't told me what the

M stands for? Mary or Martha? No." He glanced down at the shoes again as she circled to the passenger door. "Miranda, maybe? Or Melinda? Minerva? Marguerita?"

He paused while she crawled across the passenger seat and wiggled behind the wheel. Then he leaned down to continue the conversation through the window. "Mamie? Mandy? Minnie? No, on second thought, you're certainly not a mouse."

It was the third time since he'd started his litany that Mattie had bitten down on her cheek to prevent a laugh, but this time it escaped. She turned to him, distracted enough that he managed to pluck her hand off the steering wheel. The gleam in his eye warned her that if she tried to pull it away, she might not be successful. So she left it there and tried to ignore the fact that her pulse had skipped a beat and then speeded up.

There was a smile hovering around his mouth when he said, "The ring's pretty. But you're not engaged."

"That's not any—"

"Of my business. I know." Grant's smile widened as he placed her hand back on the steering wheel. "I just like to know what I might run into."

"Think about a brick wall."

He threw back his head and laughed. "Seems like I've run into one already. I can't even get you to tell me your name."

Maybe if his laugh wasn't so infectious. Maybe if amusement didn't lighten the gray of his eyes the way the sun brightened fog. Maybe then she could have stayed annoyed. But she couldn't. "You win. I was christened Moira. But only my brother dares to call me that. My father nicknamed me Mattie, and it stuck."

Grant stared openmouthed as she backed the car up and then turned it onto the highway. *Mattie!* And she hadn't been kidding. He would have bet George's recipe for blueberry buckle on it. So her name was Mattie. Spending the summer in Barclayville might prove a great deal more interesting than he'd thought

HER MIND ON OVERLOAD, Mattie skidded to a stop in the driveway of Whittaker House and crawled out the passenger door. Ghosts, curses and Grant Whittaker—especially Grant Whittaker—they'd been spinning around in her head throughout the half mile drive from George's Diner.

Grabbing her chef's toolbox from the trunk, she started up the walk. Whittaker House was her dream. From the very first day, she'd felt at home here. Just looking at the place made her smile. The two-story structure was pristine white with red shutters and shone in the sunlight. The first roses of summer were just beginning to bud on the lattice that framed the front porch.

How her father would have loved it. He'd always talked about running a restaurant in the country, far away from the dangers of urban life. How he'd hated the city, and in the end the city had taken his life. As Mattie ran her hand over the smooth paint of the banister, she thought of how strange it was that a burglar's bullet, a single act of violence so long ago, could still be affecting her life and the lives of her brother and sister. They'd both become crime fighters in the inner city, Roarke as a district attorney and Peg as a cop. And Mattie had followed the path her father would have chosen, if he'd lived.

Mattie looked out over the lawn. Her dad had been in her thoughts a lot lately. Especially since she'd failed so miserably with her inn in Maryland. Because she'd trusted Mark Brenner. Because she'd thought she loved him. But Mark was history. This time, she was going to depend on the one person she knew she could trust—herself.

If her dad were alive, he'd agree with her, she was sure. In fact, she knew exactly what he'd say to her. The same thing he'd said the day she'd come home from the playground with a black eye. "Don't worry about it, my girl. Just don't let the other guy sucker punch you more than once." And she wouldn't. This time, she was going to make her dream come true.

Grant Whittaker, curse and all, was not going to stand in her way.

After all, she hadn't let a ghost stop her!

Strains of a Chopin waltz greeted her as she crossed the porch, and the front door swung open at her approach. In the foyer, an urn of fresh flowers blocked the staircase.

How long had she known that Whittaker House was haunted? Mattie searched her memory as she hefted the urn into a niche beneath the banister. In the dining room there was an abrupt halt to the music, followed by a trill that sounded suspiciously like a giggle. Mattie couldn't help grinning as she hurried down the hallway.

The proper positioning of the urn had been in contention ever since the restaurant had opened for business. Although for the life of her, Mattie couldn't figure out why. Of course, there was the cold spot right at the top of the stairs. But the only room that was finished on the second floor was her office, so she was the only person who had any reason to go up there. Her best guess was that her ghost just had a thing about stairs.

Mattie had been aware of a presence in Whittaker House from the beginning. The signs had been subtle at first, as if the ghost was being careful not to scare her away. There was the scent of lilacs. She'd smelled them as she'd driven past on the highway. Lilacs on a rainy day in March? No doors had swung open back then. She'd just never had to use a key. And the first time she'd heard the music, she'd been asleep. The next day, she'd discovered the old harpsichord in the attic.

Mattie made her way between the tables to where it now sat in a windowed alcove. Nothing. She let her gaze move slowly around the dining room. She'd never seen a thing. And no one in Barclayville had ever breathed a word to her about the ghost. But they'd known. A series of scenes played through her mind: Lily Clemson explaining to a customer that the harpsichord had an automatic player mechanism; Ada Mae Clemson blaming the sugar-filled saltshaker on a new member of the staff.

Even George Schuler had kept the ghost's existence a secret.

But then so had she. For an entire year, she hadn't mentioned a word about her secret friend to anyone, not even to her family.

How long would she have kept the secret if Grant Whittaker hadn't spilled the beans this afternoon? Mattie turned back to the harpsichord. "I met your great-nephew today."

Nothing.

"He says everyone in town knows about you. But he doesn't believe in you."

The harpsichord was silent.

"He also told me about the curse."

When there was still no response, Mattie headed toward the kitchen. She made it to the doorway before she heard the first few bars of "Mendelssohn's Wedding March." She looked over her shoulder. "So you know about that? Except that the merry march down the aisle leads to misery for everyone in Barclayville." She frowned. "And that bothers me. I can't see someone like you leaving behind a legacy like that."

Her head began to spin again. What was the matter with her? She was actually talking to a ghost she believed in about a curse she didn't believe in. Both of which were much easier to think about than Grant Whittaker and her response to him.

What she needed was two hours in her kitchen with her mind totally focused on creating the perfect *bombe au chocolat*. Then she'd be able to sort through everything, even Grant Whittaker.

From the dining room came the strains of Chopin again, a polonaise. As the triumphant chords filled the kitchen, Mattie threw back her head and laughed. Someone was on her side.

"IF YOU WANT your son, the best advice I can give you is to grab this opportunity and run with it."

Grant turned from the window to watch his attorney pace on an expanse of Oriental carpet. A slender man with a compact, wiry build, Joel Lawson looked more like a world-class gymnast than the best child-custody lawyer in upstate New York. But the scent of leather-bound books and the view of the lake from his ninth-floor office bore testimony to Joel's success. Even more important to Grant was the fact that he had known Joel since college, and he trusted his friend's advice. Even on those occasions when he wasn't happy about it.

Joel sat for a moment on the corner of his desk. "Lisa has set up certain conditions, that's true. But nothing you can't manage. And nothing that wouldn't benefit J.D. She wants to assure herself that her son will have a stable, secure home."

"I don't have a problem with that," Grant said.

Joel gave him a steady look. "Translated, that means a house, not an apartment, a car, not a motorcycle, and you'll have to give up the consulting part of your work with the university, at least temporarily. I'd suggest you take on a full load of classes for the next few semesters."

"What other hoops does she want me to jump through before she'll give me my son?" Grant asked.

Joel sighed. "It will be easier if you don't look at it that way. I've spoken with your ex-wife's attorney twice. What I'm getting is that since she became pregnant, the new husband has been putting pressure on her to let you take custody of J.D. That way, she can devote more time to the new baby. The 'hoops,' as you call them, are one way she has of dealing with her guilt." Joel rose and met Grant's eyes squarely. "Whatever she's asking, you go one step further. And move quickly. The sooner you can convince her that you've lost your wanderlust and put down roots in the community, the better."

Wanderlust. Grant stared out the window again. His traveling had been a source of contention in their marriage right from the beginning. Though he'd cut back on them, he hadn't entirely eliminated his consulting jobs. He'd argued that the practical experience in the field made him a more effective teacher. And then there were the articles he'd published as a result of his consultations. After the divorce, he'd increased his time on the road to avoid returning to an empty apartment.

"Okay." Grant ran a hand through his hair as he walked toward his old friend. "Increasing the teaching load is no problem. And there are two other faculty members who can take over the consulting jobs. But I can't leave Barclayville for at least two months."

Joel shot him a grin. "No problem."

Grant frowned. "Won't I need to look for a house?"

"Not if you stay there." Joel moved behind his desk and pulled a document out of an open file. "Don't you own two places in Barclayville? Yes, here it is in the divorce agreement. Your family home and the mansion that your great-aunt got as an engagement gift. I'd still like to know how she managed to dump the guy and still hang on to the real estate. She must have been quite a woman." Joel glanced up from the file. "Just move into one of these houses. And that diner you're running? Any chance you could buy it?"

"No! I have no desire to settle down in Barclayville!"

"Develop one. Your ex-wife knows very well that you can change your teaching schedule at Cornell anytime you want. I'm advising you to give her every assurance you possibly can that you are committed to a business, and a community. That will spell security for your son."

Grant began to pace. "You don't understand. I don't want to raise J.D. in Barclayville." He paused. The curse had sounded lame enough when he'd explained it to Ms. Farrell earlier. How was he going to explain it to Joel?

"You can't be worried about the Whittaker Curse," Joel said with a grin. "Aren't curses like lightning? I'd say you've already been struck once."

Grant turned to stare at him. "How did—"

"The night before we graduated." Joel smiled. "You'd had quite a few beers. Don't worry. I've never told a soul. I figured you didn't really take it seriously."

"No, of course not. Logically, I know that it doesn't exist." Grant walked to a chair and gripped the back. "It had nothing to do with my mother's accident." But all he had to do was speak of it, and images flashed into his mind. He'd been five years old, standing on the porch of Whittaker House, when he'd seen his mother's car get plowed into by some teenagers speeding down the hill from the Barclay mansion. "And when my father tried to find solace in a bottle, I know that it wasn't any curse that caused that, either. But when I was a kid, it was tempting to blame something...someone. I wish I'd never heard of that curse." Shoving his hands into his pockets, Grant shrugged his shoulders, trying to relieve some of the tension. "It's ridiculous, I know. Maybe it's just the result of growing up in a town where I had the same last name as a ghost who got blamed for everybody's bad luck. I thought that I could put an end to it by closing the two houses and moving out of town."

Joel leaned back in his chair to study his friend. "I wouldn't be recommending that you move into one of those houses unless I thought it was the best thing for J.D."

"I know." Grant sat down. "I know. How long would I have to keep him in Barclayville?"

Joel waved a hand. "I don't want to know about your long-term plans. All I need is a detailed and very convincing scenario to present to your ex-wife's attorney."

Grant thought for a minute. "Lisa would never be impressed by a diner. And neither would her mother."

Joel shrugged. "Then make it one of those five-star gourmet places. You've certainly helped a lot of other people get started in the restaurant business. Put that consulting skill to work for yourself."

"There's already a fancy restaurant in Barclayville. George got me to sign a three-year lease on my old home. I don't think that the traffic will support two fine-dining establishments."

Joel leaned forward. "Time out. There's a restaurant already established in Whittaker House?"

"Yes. It's run by a young woman named Mattie Farrell, and I just happen to have the profit information for the last year, along with an expansion plan."

"Buy her out, my friend."

Grant thought of the determination he'd seen in Mattie's eyes. "I don't think she'd sell."

"Then dredge up some of that charm you had in college and make her a partnership offer she can't refuse."

Grant frowned. "I don't like being involved in anything that would keep anyone in Barclayville."

Joel sighed as he leaned over to pull a bottle of Scotch from a cabinet. "The curse again." After pouring two glasses, he pushed one toward Grant. "Tell her about it. Then you're covered in case she sues."

"I did tell her about it."

Joel took a sip of his drink and looked at his friend. "You're not involved with this woman, are you?"

"Of course not. I've got enough on my plate right now. Besides, even if I can't be struck by lightning twice, I'm not too keen on setting myself up for the possibility."

"Then what are you worried about? As her partner, you'll be right there with her to protect her from . . . bad luck. Or whatever."

Grant lifted his glass. "What if she doesn't want a partner?"

Joel touched his drink to Grant's. "Think of your son, and make her an offer she can't refuse."

2

IT WAS NEARLY midnight when Mattie saw her last dinner guests out the door. Then she went in search of the Clemson sisters. The kitchen was spotless. The lingering smells of the meals she'd prepared that night now mingled with the lemony scent of soap. Ada Mae stood at the stove stirring something.

"Hot milk!" She pointed a finger at Mattie. "No back talk. You're dead on your feet, and you need a good sleep."

At seventy-something, Ada Mae stood five foot two inches, had the compact body of a boxer and the overall attitude of a drill sergeant. Mattie had learned long ago that arguing with Ada Mae was about as productive as trying to discuss options with a steamroller as it flattened you to the ground. Since she had more important things to talk about to the Clemson sisters, she climbed onto a stool at the island in the center of the room.

"What is that?" Lily drifted in from the pantry, her royal blue caftan wafting behind her. She glanced into the pot, then pinched her nostrils delicately as she climbed onto a stool next to Mattie's. "Hot milk is for old ladies. Mattie needs a man."

Ada Mae's only response was a snort as she stirred peach brandy into the pot.

Mattie studied the two women. They'd shown up at her front door two weeks after she'd started work on Whittaker House. George had sent them to help out, they'd said, and within minutes they were stripping wallpaper and washing windows.

As sisters, they couldn't have been more different. Ada Mae with her short-cropped white hair was seventy-five percent General Patton and twenty-five percent Mary Poppins. Lily, on the other hand, was half Blanche du Bois and half Cheshire cat.

Ada Mae was single and had taught fifth grade at Barclayville's elementary school for over thirty years. She was a whirlwind of energy, while her younger sister favored inertia. Lily never stood if she could sit, never sat if she could recline. Even now, she was spreading herself and her caftan over two stools. According to Ada Mae, Lily had been married almost as often as she changed her hair color. Currently, the curls that framed her face were peach-colored, and her accent was deeply Southern.

"Drink up." Ada Mae set a steaming mug in front of Mattie.

"What did you think of Grant Whittaker?" Lily asked.

Mattie lifted the drink and blew on it while she framed her answer. What she thought of Grant Whittaker wasn't nearly as disturbing as how often she thought of him. She hadn't even been able to clear her mind of him while she was creating tonight's dessert. The image of Grant stretched out, sleeping in the hammock had interfered with her . . . focus. "Nice." The word slipped out before Mattie could stop it. "But he's going to be trouble," she added quickly.

Lily laughed and clapped her hands. "Wonderful. A woman never thinks of a man as trouble unless there's a spark."

Ada Mae glared at her sister as she spoke to Mattie. "Don't pay any attention to Lily. I want to know if he agreed to sign that lease."

"No," Mattie said. "But we're meeting again."

"Well, I hope he talks some sense into you!"

Mattie set down her mug. "He told me about the Whittaker Curse, if that's what you mean by *sense*."

"Shh!" Lily waved her hands as she glanced over her shoulder. "She'll hear you!"

Ada Mae shot her sister a killing look. "Lily—"

"He told me about the ghost, too." Mattie looked from one sister to the other. "What I'd like to know is why one of you didn't bother to tell me that my restaurant is haunted?"

"Not everyone is able to sense the presence of a spiritual entity," Lily began with another flutter of her hands.

"Pig piddle!" Ada Mae poured herself a shot of peach brandy and knocked it back. "We didn't tell you because we didn't want to scare you away."

"And you thought I didn't notice the sugar in the saltshakers, the harpsichord that plays by itself, the urn of flowers that wants to block the staircase?" Mattie asked.

"Child's play," Ada Mae said.

Lily spoke in a whisper. "Believe me, my dear, the ghost likes you. She wants you here, or you'd be gone."

"She always did have a mind of her own." Ada Mae set her glass down on the counter with a snap.

"You knew her?" Mattie glanced from one sister to the other. "What was she like?"

Lily rested her chin in her hands and sighed. "A heartbreaker. And very liberated for her time. After her brother married and moved to his wife's farm, she turned this place into a boardinghouse. A very successful one, too. She was an excellent cook. When Peter Barclay proposed, she was twenty-four. In those days, that made her an old maid."

Ada Mae sniffed. "She waited for money."

Lily shook her head. "It was the Cinderella story of the decade. The Barclays were from Manhattan. That's where their winter home was, right near Central Park. They were into banking and politics. They only came here for the summers, but some of their visitors . . ." Lily sighed. "U.S. senators and once even the governor came to Barclayville for a week. If I'd been ten years older, I'd have thrown my cap at Peter Barclay myself."

"So why did she jilt him?" Mattie asked.

"Because she changed her mind and decided to take off! Poof! She was never heard from again." Ada Mae snapped her fingers. "And since then, the whole town's been cursed with unhappy marriages. It could start all over again if you go messing around with that house."

"I don't believe it," Mattie said. "Not the ghost that I know. She wouldn't do that."

In the front of the house, a door suddenly banged against a wall. From the dining room came the sound of "Mendelssohn's Wedding March."

"What in the world?" Grabbing a frying pan, Ada Mae led the way out of the kitchen.

GRANT STEPPED CAUTIOUSLY into the foyer. He hadn't even raised his hand to knock when the door had suddenly swung open and crashed into the wall. Then the overhead light had gone out. Why in the world had he come? He hated to admit to the strong urge he'd felt to pull into the driveway of Whittaker House. He was tired. He'd already decided that whatever strategy he planned to use on Mattie Farrell would be better left until tomorrow. But his motorcycle seemed to have a will of its own. Impulses he understood, and he went with them when he was so inclined, but it was always his own choice. This felt different.

Grant glanced around the darkened hall. It had been twenty-five years since he'd set foot in this house. He'd never wanted to come back after the day that George had come for him and taken him to live over the diner. A temporary arrangement, George had said, just until Grant's father came back. But his father never had.

Grant had come to feel more at home in the diner with George than he'd ever felt in Whittaker House after his mother had died. Still, he was aware of something familiar, a smell. Lilacs?

And the music. It was a melody he'd heard before. To his surprise, he had to control the urge to turn and run.

Footsteps were hurrying from the back of the house. Overhead, the chandelier brightened, and he saw Mattie appear between the French doors at the end of the hallway. She wasn't alone. And she was beautiful. Why hadn't he noticed that before? She was dressed much the same way as before, in tailored white slacks and a jacket, but in the soft lamplight her hair gleamed more gold than red and her blue-violet eyes seem larger. Grant felt his mouth go dry. And then he felt the same pull that had made him turn into the driveway, only stronger.

Mattie paused in the doorway. *Different* was the word that came to her mind when she saw Grant. Perhaps because he was wearing clothes this time: a cream-colored suit with unstructured lines, a shirt in a soft-looking cloth, open at the neck. She could imagine what the material would feel like beneath her hands. And it wasn't only his clothes that she wanted to touch. She had taken two steps forward before she realized that she was moving.

Then Lily was floating past her down the hall. "Grant Whittaker, shame on you. You scared us half to death."

Grant found he had to put some effort into shifting his gaze from Mattie to Lily. "My apologies," he murmured. "But the door swung right open."

"It has a tendency to do that." Ada Mae pushed the door shut, then turned to Grant.

"Maybe you'd like to explain why you're paying a social visit this late at night?" Ada Mae asked.

"It's not a social visit. Ms. Farrell and I were interrupted when we were discussing business earlier today, and when I drove by and saw the lights on—"

"Business?" Ada Mae gave him a brief nod. "Well, see to it that you keep your mind on it, and talk some sense into her. C'mon, Lily." Taking her sister's arm, Ada Mae pulled her down the hall.

Grant watched the two ladies until they disappeared. "She can still make me feel like I'm in fifth grade."

Mattie laughed. "It's a special talent she has." She found herself smiling for no other reason than that she was pleased to see him. That surprised her. Even more surprising was the realization that she had been looking forward to seeing him all day. And here she stood like a gawking teenager when he'd said that he'd come on business.

"Come into the parlor," she invited. She turned to lead the way and found herself blocked by the urn. When she gripped the sides and pulled, it stuck.

"Let me," Grant said, lifting it easily. "Where?"

"Under the banister. Not that it will stay there long."

When Grant straightened, Mattie met his eyes squarely. "Your great-aunt prefers it to block the stairs. We have this little battle at least once a day."

When Grant stared at her, she hurried on, "I don't want any misunderstanding, and I'm afraid I left you with the wrong impression this afternoon. About the ghost, I mean. Of course, I was choking at the time. But I've met her, sort of. Until you mentioned her, I didn't know that anyone else in town knew about her, even though they all did. Do."

He was still staring at her as if she'd sprouted horns. He also looked exhausted. Mattie thought of the trip he'd just made and the reason for it and drew him with her into the parlor.

"I'm sure you didn't stop by to hear me babble on about a ghost," she said as she moved behind the antique cabinet that served as a bar. "Would you like wine, beer, something stronger...?"

"Beer, please," Grant said. She had led him into a small room that had been the parlor when he'd lived in the house. It hadn't been nearly as inviting then. Honey-colored oak floors gleamed around the edges of a faded carpet that looked familiar. He moved between two chintz-covered sofas that flanked the fireplace to study the ancient portrait hanging over the mantel. A family portrait. The mother and father looked pleased as punch with the kids—a girl sat on the arm of a sofa with her hands folded demurely in her lap and a mischievous glint in her eyes; the boy stood stiffly at her side, looking bored to death and ready to bolt.

When Mattie handed him the glass, he asked, "Where did you find that?"

"In the attic."

He toasted the portrait before taking a sip of his beer. "An ironic tribute to a happy family—the last time the Whittakers had one to boast about, no doubt. I wouldn't be at all surprised if the poker-faced kid next to the girl is my grandfather. I looked a lot like him when I was that age. He grew up in this house."

"Then the girl is your great-aunt." Mattie took a step toward the portrait. "I've thought for a long time that she's 'my' ghost. What's her name?"

Grant stared at her. "You don't know, do you?"

"I told you. The first time I've talked to anyone about her is tonight."

"Her name was Mattie Whittaker."

It was Mattie's turn to stare. He wasn't joking. She shifted her gaze to the portrait as a cold finger traced her spine. *Mattie.* Is that why she'd felt drawn to the house from the very first time she'd seen it? Why she felt certain that the ghost—Mattie—was her friend? Is that why she'd felt so at home here?

No. It was just a coincidence. She certainly didn't believe in reincarnation, although she'd never believed in ghosts before, either.

"Sit down." Grant pushed her down on the nearest sofa. He'd never seen anyone lose color so fast. He shot a glance over his shoulder at the likeness of his great-aunt. Then he moved to the bar and poured brandy into a snifter. "Here." He pressed the drink into her hand, shrugged out of his jacket and draped it around her shoulders. Then he knelt so he could see her eyes. To his relief, they were clear and focused. There was no trace of fear.

"Someone should have told me."

Grant held her still when she tried to rise. "Drink first. You're white as a . . ."

"Ghost?" She finished for him. She took a swallow of brandy. It burned its way to her stomach and she drew in a deep breath. *Mattie.* She glanced up at the portrait again. She had nothing to fear from Mattie Whittaker. Of that much she was sure.

"You really believe she haunts this place, don't you?" Grant asked as he rose and shifted his gaze to the portrait.

"I believe she's here. Didn't you ever sense something when you were living here?"

Grant shook his head.

"You must have smelled the lilacs," Mattie said.

"The house has always smelled of lilacs."

"It's her." She got up, paced to the fireplace and perched restlessly on the arm of the sofa. "This morning you wanted me to believe in the curse. But you don't believe that your aunt might still be present in this house. That doesn't make sense."

Grant sat down across from her. "I never wanted to believe in the ghost. Everyone else in town did. Especially my father. He blamed her for my mother's death and everything bad that ever happened to him. If she'd married Peter Barclay, we would have been living on easy street. Easy street. That's what he'd say whenever he'd get to the bottom of a bottle."

Reaching for his beer, Grant looked at the portrait again, and for a moment the thought was clear in his mind that Mattie Whittaker understood why he denied her existence. She understood how it was for a little boy who'd been abandoned by both his mother and father. How could he trust his great-aunt?

Uncomfortable, Grant took a quick sip of beer and shifted his gaze to Mattie Farrell. She was sitting on the arm of the sofa with her hands folded in her lap exactly the way Mattie Whittaker was posed in the portrait. For one quick second, he had the distinct feeling he was outnumbered. And then ruthlessly he shoved the feelings aside. This was ridiculous. He hadn't come here to dig up any "ghosts" from his past. He'd come to discuss business with the very real woman who was sitting across from him.

With a smile, he leaned back against the cushions. "I still don't want to believe in her. I'd prefer to think there are logical explanations for what you've experienced. I believe in what I can see." He paused to let his gaze move over Mattie. "And in what I can touch."

Touch. What was it about the man? He only had to look at her that way and say the word, and she was wondering what it would be like to be touched by him. Mattie recalled how much she'd wanted to touch him when she'd first seen him in the hammock and then again in the foyer. She found herself staring at his hands as he reached for his glass of beer. He had nice hands. Large, and his fingers were long and elegant. She watched them close around the glass. Dimly, she was aware that he was saying something. Her own hands closed into fists as she forced her gaze back to his face. "Hmm?"

He sipped the beer, then smiled. "I believe in what I can taste, too. Don't you?"

"Yes," she said and was surprised at how clear the word sounded in the room. Gathering her scattered thoughts, she went on, "But shouldn't the same rules apply to the curse? You claim that it's supported by facts. But couldn't all the failed marriages in Barclayville have some explanation other than the theory that your great-aunt wanted to ruin everyone's lives?"

Admiration. He couldn't help feeling it at the way she'd turned his own argument against him. And she'd given him the perfect opening to tell her he'd changed his mind about the lease. But he hesitated. Curses and ghosts aside, J.D. had to come first. Still, he found himself saying, "I meant what I said in the diner. You might be better off if you left Barclayville."

Mattie lifted her chin. "I'm staying."

Grant gave her a brief nod. His glass had left a damp imprint on the table, and he rubbed at it with his fingers. He and Joel had rehearsed this little speech over dinner. Everything he was saying was the truth. "I wasn't fair to you this afternoon. I do a lot of consulting work for hotels and inns, a lucrative spin-off of my job at Cornell. I never make a business decision without studying the plans and visiting the site. I read the papers that you left with me, and I'm impressed." He took a sip of his drink. It tasted as bitter as a lie.

"You've changed your mind about signing the lease?"

"I'll need to take a look at the place before I decide."

"I could give you a tour tomorrow."

Grant didn't respond right away. Joel had advised him to take it slowly. His change of mind and his offer of a partnership would be much more convincing if he allowed Mattie to persuade him. He reached for the beer and decided against it. "I'm not sure I can get an engineer here that quickly."

Mattie waved a hand. "They won't find any structural damage. I've already had it inspected. George has done an exceptional job for you. The Barclay mansion is in fine shape considering how long it's been vacant. How about one o'clock?"

"Fine." Grant rose. "But I'll have to have a report from my own engineer."

"Absolutely." Mattie handed him his jacket, then tried to contain her excitement as she followed him out of the room. It wouldn't do at all to jump up and down for joy.

She almost walked into his back when he stopped to move the urn of flowers again. When he turned around, she said, "She's going to make a believer out of you yet."

"It'll take more than a moving urn. I'm going to have my engineer check the slant of the floor."

"It's flat. You'll see."

What he saw was Mattie Farrell, her eyes bright with amusement, her chin lifted in determination. It suddenly occurred to him that whatever his own reservations were about the existence of his great-aunt's spirit, Mattie believed. And she'd been living in the same house with Mattie Whittaker for a year, while creating a successful business, to boot. That had required both courage and vision.

He reached out to tuck a curl behind her ear. "Even if you were to suddenly convince me that there are two Matties here right now—" he ran his finger back along her cheek and tapped her chin lightly "—I'd still choose you."

Mattie felt the trail of heat his finger left, long after he'd closed the door behind him.

THE NEXT AFTERNOON, Grant walked up the long driveway that curved from the main road to the Barclay mansion. Hannibal had persuaded him to leave the bike behind by settling himself in an immovable mound behind the motorcycle's rear wheel. He hadn't gotten far on foot before the dog was lumbering along at his side.

The moment the mansion came into view, Grant stopped. The main section had stood for well over a hundred years. The Barclays had added on a second and third story, complete with a widow's walk that rose like a steeple against the sky. The air smelled of grass baked in the sun, and lilacs. No, not lilacs. It had to the honeysuckle that grew wild in the tangle of weeds that had once been a lawn.

In the clear light of day, he found it easier to keep ghosts and curses in their place, right next to Santa Claus and the tooth fairy. He was definitely going to have his engineer check the slope of the floor in Whittaker House where the urn seemed to possess the power of locomotion.

As far as the curse went, Mattie Farrell had made a good point. How many failed marriages among the residents of Barclayville could be blamed entirely on a curse? Not his own certainly. An unplanned pregnancy was not the best basis for a marriage, and Lisa had quickly fixed her eye on greener pastures. The real victim of the divorce had been J.D. And now at five years of age, his son was about to have his home life disrupted once more. Never again, Grant promised himself.

He climbed the front steps and watched Hannibal arrange himself so that he blocked the front door. Grant turned to take in the view. To his right, the valley was a patchwork quilt of planted fields working their way steadily toward harvest. Straight ahead, down a gently sloping hill was Whittaker House, hidden by apple trees. The two houses were less than a few city blocks apart. It would be easy to cut a path through the orchard and install gaslights. It would make a nice after-dinner walk.

Grant frowned. Already he was beginning to think of Mattie's plan as a reality, and it wouldn't do to let her think that. He shoved his hands into his pockets. The deception, small as it was, grated on him. Today, he'd put an end to it. As soon as he had her signature on a partnership agreement.

Just then he saw her at the edge of the orchard, striding across the weed-covered lawn. She was dressed the same as when he'd first seen her, in white jeans and a shirt, with a red pouch strapped around her waist. Today she wore sneakers. It occurred to him as he watched her walk in that quick determined way she had that Ms. M. Farrell might end up being harder to deal with than all the ghosts and curses of Barclayville.

For one thing, she was an astute businesswoman. Of course, he couldn't help admiring that. The plan she'd given him and he'd passed on to Joel was as well prepared as any he'd seen. He'd also learned, to his great surprise, that Mattie Farrell hadn't chosen to open a restaurant in Barclayville on a whim—or because a ghost was making her do it. She'd done her research. Whittaker House was within an hour's drive of six upstate colleges or universities and four good-size cities. Barclayville *was* an excellent location for a country inn.

Her business acumen wasn't the only thing that surprised him. He couldn't quite shake off the strange feeling he'd had the night before, in Whittaker House, that he was losing control. He leaned against the porch railing. The truth was, he was attracted to Mattie Farrell. Strongly attracted.

There was J.D. to consider, though, and Mattie Farrell played a very important part in the strategy that he and Joel Lawson had worked out. It would be wiser if he kept his mind on business. He watched the sun make a halo of Mattie's hair as she sidestepped a patch of thorns. Then again, life was short. Maybe he couldn't afford *not* to mix business with pleasure.

"Am I late?" Mattie asked as she climbed the porch steps.

"Hannibal and I were early."

The dog shook himself and sneezed as Grant dragged him away from the door.

"Why does he always choose a doorway to nap in?" she asked.

"My guess is, he likes to keep track of comings and goings. He was a pretty good watchdog once."

Mattie's eyebrows shot up.

Grant grinned as he took out a key and twisted it in the lock. "He's also afraid to be left behind."

"That I can believe," she said as Hannibal nudged her through the door then resettled himself over the threshold. She walked briskly through the foyer and started up the stairs.

Halfway to the second floor, Grant took her arm. "Are you always in such a hurry?"

"I don't like to waste time."

"I'll have to keep that in mind."

Mattie shifted her gaze to his hand. "And I've been climbing stairs by myself since I was two years old."

"These stairs are pretty steep. And as long as my name's on the deed, I'd just as soon you didn't fall."

He kept his hand on her arm the rest of the way up. Turning at the top of the staircase, Mattie disengaged herself. "They may be steep, but they're lovely. The banister is hand-carved." She withdrew a flashlight from the pouch at her waist and aimed it at the post. "You can tell because the space between the markings isn't always the same. So the carving wasn't done by a machine."

Stooping over, Grant ran his hand along the base. "There are some scratches here."

With a frown, Mattie aimed her flashlight closer. "I hadn't noticed. But they're not deep. I'm sure they can be fixed. There's surprisingly little vandalism, considering the length of time the house has been vacant. Is it really the curse that's kept everyone out for fifty years?"

"I think it was a combination of fear and lack of finances. Supposedly, the Barclay family moved the furniture out and closed the place down after Mattie jilted Peter, and it wasn't until Peter Barclay died that my grandfather learned Peter had deeded it over to Mattie as an engagement gift. None of my relatives had the money to furnish it, much less do anything else with it. But the curse can probably be credited with keeping the vandals out."

"Well, at least it's had one good effect." Mattie led the way down the hall.

"You seem to be very familiar with the place," he said to her back.

"I've been through it a few times."

"Trespassing?" he asked.

She paused in front of a carved oak door and shot him a glance. "There was no sign. And the French doors to the front parlor are easy to open. Don't tell me you grew up in Barclayville and never once broke in?"

Grant smiled. "A few Halloweens I came up here with some friends. We never stayed long."

"Did you smell lilacs?"

"No."

They reached for the doorknob at the same time, and for a moment Grant's hand covered hers. Trying to ignore the ribbon of fire that shot up her arm, she threw the weight of her shoulder into the door, shoving it open.

"This was probably the master bedroom," she said, leading the way across the room. She pointed out the porcelain tiles that framed the fireplace and the two windows that provided a view of the valley, and watched Grant as he ran his fingers over the carved mantel, disturbing some cobwebs. He looked relaxed, perfectly at ease, while she felt wired.

It was high time she faced the fact that something about the man got to her. Maybe it was the way his eyes would linger on her at times—persistent, almost expectant. Or perhaps it was that half-amused look that told her he knew exactly what it was he was expecting. And that it wouldn't be long before she would, too.

Well, she didn't have time for whatever it was he had in mind. She had a business to expand, and all she wanted was to sell him on her idea. She pushed through a door into a tiny room adjoining the bedroom.

Grant stretched his arms out and touched both walls. His eyes were laughing when they met hers. "How much do you want to bet that this is where Mr. Barclay had to sleep when he and Mrs. Barclay had a tiff?"

Mattie pressed her lips tightly together to keep from smiling as he turned and opened another door leading to the hallway.

"Or it could have been where Mr. Barclay made his escape to keep a tryst with the maid."

This time, Mattie had to the laugh. "Is that the kind of reputation the Barclay men had? No wonder your great-aunt left old Peter in the lurch."

Grant shrugged. "Maybe. I have no idea." He glanced back at the room. "But it does make you wonder."

"Wonder about a bathroom," she said, heading down the hall. "That's a perfect spot for one. I'm hoping to find space for four more." She opened another door. "This suite has even more potential than the master bedroom, don't you think?"

Grant walked over to the black marble fireplace. The wall above it was covered with fragile-looking, faded paper, stained with smoke. When he turned, Mattie waved him toward the window.

"See that gully over there?"

He followed the direction in which she was pointing. "You mean, the big hole that backs into the orchard?"

She smiled. "You got it. I was thinking that big hole could make a pond. In the evening, it could be lit by gaslights. In the winter, it could be a skating rink."

Grant studied the slope of the land. The gully was about one hundred yards long at its base and perhaps fifty wide. He wasn't a landscape architect, but as Mattie described what she wanted, he had no trouble picturing what the area might look like.

"Very effective," he said. "I learned from reading your two-year plan that you're a good businesswoman. But you have imagination and vision, too. I'm impressed."

Mattie was surprised at the quick surge of pleasure she felt, hearing his words. "Thank you."

"No need. Someone with less vision would have wanted to install a swimming pool."

"It would spoil the feel of the place," she said. "Besides, people can get that at a motel. I want this place to be different. No tennis courts, either. But I would allow a gazebo."

"For *al fresco* dining?" he asked with an arched eyebrow.

She gave him her sweetest smile. "Or very secret little trysts."

Grant laughed. Resting his hand on the window frame, he studied her for a minute. "You're a rare one, Mattie Farrell." Enough sunlight was making its way through the years of grime on the window to bring out the red highlights in her hair. He reached over to tuck a strand behind her ear; it was cool to his touch, in contrast to the color that promised such heat. "You never did tell me why your father decided to nick-name you Mattie."

"It was partly because he expected another son. After my brother, Roarke, he must have thought he was on a roll, and he wanted to name me after his father, Matthew Farrell. Old Mat was quite a famous boxer in his day." As she spoke, Mattie led the way to the hall. "When I turned out to be a girl, my mother absolutely refused to name me Mathilda. Moira was a compromise, but my father always called me Mattie. On the day I came home from kindergarten with a black eye, he said it was a sign that he was right, and after that my mother gave up."

They were walking shoulder to shoulder down the hall. "You said your brother still calls you Moira?" Grant repeated the name, testing it on his tongue. "Moira."

Mattie pinned him with a warning look. "Only because he's my brother. And before you get any ideas, that day in kindergarten, the other kid lost his two front teeth."

Grant ran his tongue experimentally over his. "Mattie, then," he agreed amiably. He took her arm and walked with her into the next room. "What are your plans for this?"

She told him, and then directed him through a maze of hallways and more rooms, doing her best to keep her mind on her goal and her distance from Grant Whittaker. Every time she turned, though, he was there . . . with a hand on her arm or at the small of her back, to guide her over a loose floorboard or down a few steps. How many times would she experience that little tingle of awareness, that arrow of heat, before she got used to it? Would she ever?

She saved the main parlor for last. "The other rooms on the first floor can be used for meetings, but this would make a great library," she said. "I won't have enough money at first. It'll have to wait, along with the bedrooms on the third floor, but eventually I plan to stock the shelves with old books from auctions and garage sales. Really old books that can't be found anywhere else."

Grant could picture it perfectly as he walked to the French doors and looked out. Suddenly, he didn't see the lawn overgrown with weeds, he saw a pond with skaters on it. Later, they would come in to drink hot chocolate or mulled wine in front of the fire. The room itself had cracks in the plaster, peeling wallpaper but Grant only saw what Mattie was describing. And more... Some evenings they would be here alone. Mattie would be at the fireplace as she was now, dressed in something white and flowing. The same feeling he'd experienced in the foyer of Whittaker House the night before moved through him. With a frown, Grant gave his head a shake. Fantasies were nice, but it was reality he had to keep in mind if he was going to do the right thing for J.D.

"Grant?"

"Hmm?"

"The cellar's next," Mattie said as she started for the foyer.

"You have plans for that, too?"

"Not really. But it's something your engineer will want to see."

Hannibal lumbered to his feet as they walked past him. Flashlight in hand, Mattie led the way down the steep, narrow stairs. She tried to ignore the ominous creaks, and breathed a sigh of relief when she reached the bottom. Though she wouldn't have admitted it to anyone, the cellar bothered her a little, and she was glad to have Grant with her. To her surprise, she found that the dog had followed them.

"What's with him?" she asked. "I thought he only guarded doors."

"Maybe he thinks this is some kind of escape route. Is there another way out?"

"Not that I know of. Except for the windows." They were small and dirty and broke the long expanse of stone wall at intervals about three feet over their heads.

"May I?" Grant reached for the flashlight. It did little more to pierce the darkness than did the light struggling through the windows. He began to feel his way along the wall.

"You never came down here that Halloween?" Mattie asked.

Grant chuckled. "We always thought we'd proven our manhood if we could run through the front parlor and race back out again." As his eyes grew accustomed to the darkness, he could see that the room was cavernous. "If you've been down here alone, my hat's off to you."

Mattie stayed close behind him as he made his way along the wall. "Since we're being totally honest, I'll admit that I chose a day when my family was here. I knew that my brother, a fearless D.A., wouldn't let me come down here alone. His wife, C.J., is pregnant, so he wouldn't allow her on the stairs. My mother's excuse was that she didn't want to leave C.J. alone."

Grant turned to her then. "So you're not quite as fearless as you seem to be."

They were standing very close. So close she caught his scent. He smelled of sun and fresh air, and something else very male. They were close enough that she could feel his warmth. But even more than the heat, she felt a tugging, a pull that seemed to reach to her very center. Though she wanted to back away, or even bolt up the stairs, she stayed where she was.

When Grant reached to pull a cobweb from her hair, she felt a little shock wave right down to her toes. Even then she didn't step away. As always when she had a problem, she was going to understand it and then solve it.

Grant watched her. Her chin was tilted, half in defiance, half in determination. Even in the dim light, he could see her feelings in her eyes. He felt the same pull of desire that he'd felt ever since he'd met her. He ran his hand from her hair down to the edge of her jaw then slowly back again. Her skin was as soft as he'd imagined. Her lips would be, too. He'd wondered what she would taste like long enough.

He lowered his head and his lips brushed against hers. Mattie couldn't have moved even if she'd wanted to. She could no longer feel her legs. All she could feel was her heart hammering against her chest and the pressure of his fingers against the back of her neck. All she could hear in the quiet of the cellar was the sound of each breath they drew.

And then he kissed her.

Intensity. Mattie had never felt anything quite so intense. She was sure she would remember the sensation forever—the pressure of his lips, the shape of his mouth, the texture of his tongue. And his taste. Hot, dark and forbidden . . .

Her hands clenched into fists, she moved closer and found the heat she'd expected, and more. It poured into her like hot wax, melting everything in its path. Her hands went slack at her sides, and with her mouth alone, she met his demands.

The heat grew. Even her heart seemed to dissolve, when only seconds ago it had been trying to pound itself out of her chest. If it hadn't been for the pressure of his fingers on the back of her neck, she was sure she would have slipped to the floor. Any minute now, she was going to turn into steam and float away.

Before she did, Grant's hands ran over her, pressing, molding, until she was held hard against him, gripping him and moaning his name.

Stunned. That's how she made him feel. She couldn't have been more effective if she'd knocked him out cold. And that was before the heat hit him, the fire he'd known was smoldering within her from the beginning. But it was far beyond what he'd imagined—blazing, so intense. It triggered a need so sharp, so rough-edged, so desperate that it sliced right through him.

Hannibal began to bark. Loud staccato barks, followed by a muffled growl.

Grant kept a tight hold on Mattie as they moved toward the dog, who was pawing at a pile of bricks that had fallen loose from the wall. He aimed the flashlight at the hole just behind the fallen bricks. Mattie took a steadying breath and said, "Don't worry. The foundation's not crumbling. This is an old fireplace. It must have been used for cooking once. See these stones?" She lifted her arm and Grant followed her hand with the light. "This is really what I wanted you to see. It seems a shame that someone bricked this arch up."

Hannibal barked again. This time, the sound was muffled because he'd poked his head into the hole. More bricks crumbled under his assault.

Grant grabbed the dog and tugged. Hannibal ignored him and continued to work on the wall.

"Hannibal!" Grant shifted his weight and pulled again. On his next tug, Hannibal came out, along with a small land-slide of bricks. Triumphant, the animal dropped a bone at Mattie's feet and barked.

Grant aimed the light at the bone, then leaned over to get a better look. If it hadn't been so white, he would have thought it was a long stick. While they stood there staring at it, Hannibal presented them with another bone, this one shorter and curved.

"It looks like a rib," Mattie whispered.

Hannibal had his head in the hole again. This time, there was no mistaking what he pulled out.

Grant stepped in front of Mattie to block her view. It had taken him only a second to see it was a human skull.

He was drawing Mattie toward the stairs when she said, "It was a skull."

"Yeah." The lie he'd considered telling would have been short-lived.

At the foot of the stairs, she stopped. "The dog. We can't—"

"He'll follow," Grant assured her, pulling her along.

Halfway up the stairs, Mattie resisted again. "We can't leave her."

"*Her?*" Grant asked.

"Didn't you smell the lilacs? That skull belongs to your great-aunt Mattie."

3

MATTIE SAT on the front porch of the Barclay mansion, her arms clasped tightly around her knees. It had been two hours since she and Grant had called the police from the phone in Whittaker House. Most of that time they'd spent waiting for the sheriff.

It turned out that Sheriff Delaney was an old classmate of Grant's from elementary-school days, and once he'd heard their story, he'd notified the state police headquarters and called in a crew to dismantle the bricks that blocked the old fireplace.

It was quiet except for the drone of insects and Hannibal's snoring. The dog had picked his usual spot in front of the door. The clang of the pickaxes had stopped about twenty minutes ago.

"Hannibal!"

Through the screen door, she saw Grant nudge the dog out of the way. Sheriff Delaney followed him out onto the porch.

"Mac" was what Grant called him, and in his denim jacket and jeans, the man looked more like a cowboy than a law-enforcement officer. His hair was bleached by the sun, his skin tanned. The only things missing were a ten-gallon hat and a six-gun holster. Mattie wondered if he wore a gun beneath his jacket.

"We're almost finished here, ma'am. The remains are bagged, and they're packing everything into a box. I'll drive it over to the state lab myself. In the meantime, try to put it out of your mind. Based on what we found, I'd say whatever happened here, happened a long time ago."

"Will the lab be able to make a positive identification?" Mattie asked.

"Of whom?" Mac's eyes narrowed.

"Mattie thinks that we just discovered my great-aunt," Grant explained.

"Any particular reason?" Mac asked.

"I smelled lilacs," Mattie began.

"It's a long story," Grant said when the sheriff looked at him curiously. "Nothing based on facts."

Mac nodded. "Well, it's amazing what our labs can do now to pinpoint the age of a skeleton. We can even tell how long it's been buried. And there's always medical and dental records. In any case—" Mac patted his pocket "—I'd like you to stop by on Monday to sign a formal report. You remember the way to Mason's Corners."

Grant was surprised. "You're not here in town?"

"Barclayville doesn't have its own sheriff anymore. To save on taxes, a few of the towns are sharing services. Mason's Corners is centrally located." One of Mac's crew hailed him.

"Mac! We're all done."

Mac Delaney waved as his crew filed past the side of the porch.

Mattie moved to the railing to watch the men load a box into the sheriff's car. Mac and Grant were still talking.

"How long you back for, Mac?"

"Hard to say. I signed on temporarily because I needed a little vacation from my job in New York. Can't complain about the pace here, or the stress, either. How 'bout you? You're the one person I never thought I'd see in this town again."

"We took a blood oath, as I recall," Grant said.

Mac laughed. "Senior-prom night."

"A blood oath?" Mattie interrupted.

"Grant's blood," Mac explained. "He always ended up losing some whenever we decided to go out with the same girl. I usually ended up with a cracked rib." He rubbed his side as he started down the steps.

"Mac, can you keep a lid on this thing with the skeleton?" Grant asked. "Mattie has plans to expand her restaurant and use the Barclay mansion for overnight accommodations. If a lot of rumors start flying..."

Mac turned to Mattie with a look of respect. "Brave girl. Taking on a haunted house, and now this place. I wish you luck. It's about time someone tried to breathe new life into this town." He turned back to Grant. "My crew is local. By tonight, everyone within a twenty-mile radius will know about the bones, but don't worry, they won't talk to outsiders. Once the investigation starts, though, I won't have as much control, and the press might get wind of it."

"Investigation?" Mattie echoed.

"There's not much chance that Great-Aunt Mattie, or whoever it is, got in that fireplace by herself. And whoever did the masonry work is not going to be happy with today's discovery. The statute of limitations never runs out on murder."

NEITHER MATTIE NOR GRANT spoke until Mac's car was disappearing down the driveway. Then Mattie began to pace across the length of the porch. "I hadn't even thought. It never occurred to me what all this would mean."

Grant studied her. It was a pleasure, as always, to watch her walk—quickly, purposefully, as if the movement itself would give her the answers she was seeking. He could tell by the way she put her hands on her hips, and by the tiny line that had appeared on her forehead that she was thinking, sorting things out.

Odd that he already knew so much about her. He knew that the white clothes she wore and the neat way she braided her hair, both presented a cool and tempting contrast to the fire that lay beneath the surface.

With an effort, he dragged his attention back to what she was saying.

"I never told anyone about the ghost, not even my family. My brother probably would've hired some ghost buster to dehaunt the place. And I was worried about customers finding out that Whittaker House was haunted, that it would scare them away. But now . . ." Mattie raised her hands and dropped them.

He'd never seen her at such a loss before. "If you advertise properly," he said, "you'll be booked solid on Halloween."

She stared at him for a second, then began to laugh. She laughed until she was doubled over, with her hands holding her sides. When she could finally catch a breath, she said, "That's not funny." Then she doubled over again, giggling uncontrollably.

Grant went to her thinking that one thing he hadn't known was how much pleasure it would give him to make her laugh. Taking her hands, he drew her upright. When he tilted her chin up, he saw tears in her eyes. She was right. It hadn't been that funny. "Mattie—"

"I'm all right. Really," she said. "I'm not getting hysterical." She managed a smile. "It helped to laugh. Ever since we found her, I haven't been able to catch a breath."

"We don't know for sure that it's her."

"I *know* it is," she insisted. "And she was only twenty-four. That's the real tragedy. To have your whole life snatched away from you. My father was thirty-eight when he was shot and killed in a burglary. It's not right. We have to find out what happened."

Grant couldn't help thinking of his mother as he drew Mattie closer. To lose a parent because of an accident was bad enough, but to lose one to a violent crime . . . he could only imagine. "Mac's a good man."

"We've got to help him."

"You're a chef. I'm a college professor."

Mattie raised her eyebrows.

"All right. College professor slash restaurant consultant slash whatever it is I'm doing running George's Diner for the summer. My point is, we ought to leave it to the professionals. Mac's on leave from the New York City Police Department. When he goes back, he'll be up for captain. And he's good at his job."

"I still think—"

Grant placed a finger over her lips. Later, he would think about how right it felt to be holding her. "You think too much. You can't do everything. You have a restaurant to run tonight, plans to make for this place."

"You don't understand. We can't just leave it to the police to handle this. No matter how good they are, they can make mistakes. The man who murdered my father never went to jail."

"Mattie, I . . ." Grant couldn't think of anything to say. Pulling her into his arms, he ran a hand up her back and held her close. When she touched him in return, he felt something warm move through him. It wasn't at all as he'd imagined a few moments ago. There was no punch, no explosion. He simply didn't want to let her go.

Mattie knew she should pull away, but it felt so natural to have his arms around her, to hear the thudding of his heart, so sure and steady. For a moment, she allowed herself to relax. This felt so right. Just for a minute, she promised herself. She couldn't remember feeling this secure since she was a child, before her father had died. It felt different from before, when Grant had kissed her in the cellar, and those soul-shattering sensations had ripped through her. She dragged her thoughts back to Great-Aunt Mattie, and the issue at hand. "Do you see why I don't want to leave this up to Mac?"

"But how can you hope to solve a fifty-year-old murder, if that's what it turns out to be? And is that more important than expanding Whittaker House?"

She stepped away from him. "According to you, Mattie has been blamed for a curse that has driven everyone under seventy out of Barclayville. And that's not fair. She didn't jilt Peter Barclay. Someone murdered her to prevent that wedding from taking place."

He wasn't convinced. "Even if you're right, I can't see what we can do about it."

"We can lift the curse by making sure that everyone knows the truth."

Grant suddenly smiled. "Lift the curse? Last night you were trying to convince me to believe in the ghost. Now, you're believing in the curse."

After studying him for a minute, she shook her head. "We're very different, you and I."

Grant's smile widened. "That's what will make it so interesting."

"What?"

"What's going to happen between us."

Mattie's chin lifted. "The only thing that's going to happen between us is business."

"You know what they say? By any other name, a rose still smells as sweet."

For the life of her, Mattie couldn't think of an appropriate reply, so she descended the porch steps and stalked away across the weed-covered lawn.

"IT'S LATE," Ada Mae said, the moment Mattie stepped through the back door. "We were worried."

"I had a meeting with Grant." Mattie glanced at her watch and realized it was almost five. She'd been running off schedule ever since she'd met him. Grabbing her chef's jacket from a hook, she slipped it on then fumbled with the buttons.

"The Robinsons called," Ada Mae said. "They can't make it until six-thirty."

The harpsichord began to play in the dining room. Mattie jumped, and Ada Mae stepped back to take a good look at her. "It's just Lily practicing," she said. "What's the matter?" She narrowed her eyes. "It's *her*, isn't it?"

Mattie moved past Ada Mae. "C'mon," she said. "I have to tell Lily, too."

For the second time that day, Mattie related the story of her meeting with Grant at the Barclay mansion and of how Hannibal's digging had uncovered the bones of Mattie Whittaker. It wasn't as difficult as it had been with Sheriff Delaney.

Lily leaned close and spoke in a whisper. "You're sure it was Mattie?"

"I know it's her." Mattie glanced down at her hands. She'd been gripping them together so tightly they hurt. Very carefully, she drew them apart.

Ada Mae pulled out a chair and pushed Mattie into it. "Sit down." Then she turned and disappeared into the front parlor.

"Why doesn't she like Mattie Whittaker?" Mattie asked.

"Ada Mae's never forgiven her for hurting George Schuler." Lily sat down next to Mattie and began to adjust the folds of her purple chiffon dress. "He had a terrible crush on Mattie when we were in high school. Puppy love. She was nine years older than him. Still, he took it very hard when she became engaged."

"And Ada Mae's holding a grudge?"

"She thinks George is still carrying a torch for Mattie Whittaker." At Mattie's incredulous look, she went on, "He took Grant in and raised him when Grant's father left. He's looked after Mattie's houses for all these years. Oh, legally they're Grant's now, but originally they both belonged to Mattie."

Ada Mae came into the room carrying a tray with three glasses. "Brandy," she said as she served them. "Drink up. We have a long night ahead of us."

Ada Mae tossed hers back while Lily and Mattie sipped theirs, then she began to move between the tables, pausing at each one to check the saltshakers. Ada Mae had always blamed the staff, never a ghost, for the sugar that seemed magically to get into the saltshakers.

Mattie reached for the shaker on her table and sprinkled some in her hand. It was a ritual they went through every night before any guests arrived. But tonight, Mattie's mind wasn't on the task and she dropped her hand to the table without tasting any of the granules. "Lily, what kind of reputation did Peter Barclay have with women?"

Lily sighed. "He was everything a woman dreamed about. Handsome as sin. And rich."

"Were there any rumors that he ran around? Had affairs?"

"Not that I know of," Lily replied with a slight frown. "But there was gossip that he was in love with someone else about five years before he got engaged to Mattie. A girl named Rachel Williams. Now, if he'd ended up marrying her, it would have been a real Cinderella story. She worked in the kitchen at the mansion. But he went overseas to fight in the war, and Rachel moved out of town." Lily turned to Mattie. "He never did marry, you know. His sister, Amelia, lived with him and acted as his hostess after he was elected to the Senate. She didn't marry, either."

"I found three filled with sugar," Ada Mae said as she joined them and proceeded to test the one Mattie had tried earlier. "Make that four."

"So neither of the Barclays married. Is that the way the curse affects that family?" Mattie asked.

"Shh!" Lily's voice dropped to a whisper again. "It's not good to talk about the curse. It gives it more power."

Mattie stood up. "I think it's already had quite enough power over this town. And the wrong person's been blamed!"

"What do you mean?" Ada Mae asked the question, but both sisters were staring at her.

"Mattie Whittaker never jilted Peter Barclay. Somebody killed her to prevent the wedding, and I intend to find out who."

WITH A FULL MOON pouring light on it, Whittaker House didn't look haunted. In fact, from where Grant stood on the side of the highway with Hannibal slumped at his feet, it looked welcoming. It was hard to imagine that this was the same place George Schuler had rescued him from twenty-five years ago.

He owed George a lot. The man had done more for him than take him in and raise him. George had also taught him a business that Grant still enjoyed. He might have gotten away from Barclayville, but much of his work both in and out of the classroom still centered around providing people with a home away from home, whether it was for the length of a meal or longer.

Mattie Farrell, too, had done a good job with Whittaker House. She'd changed it for the better. Grant was confident that she could work the same magic on the Barclay mansion. In fact, he was looking forward to working with her.

He could still recall the joy of looking at the first resort he'd been a part of creating. It had been a small country inn in

Virginia. Every year, he tried to visit. With the expansion of Whittaker House, he'd be even more than just a consultant—this time he'd be a part of it.

A few minutes ago, Mattie Farrell had turned the light on in the parlor, and Grant had seen her framed briefly in the window.

Ever since then, he'd been debating whether or not to disturb her. He could always claim business as his excuse; the partnership agreement that Joel had drawn up was in his pocket.

He glanced at his watch. It was late. Twelve-thirty. It had been a busy night at the diner. Serving dinner on weekend nights was George's way of providing a social outlet for Barclayville's senior citizens, and Grant had continued the tradition. More often than not, local gossip triumphed over cuisine.

Mrs. Deitz had brought the news that a skeleton had been discovered at the Barclay mansion. No one had talked of anything else for the rest of the evening.

But it hadn't been business that had drawn him to Whittaker House tonight, nor had it been some extra-earthly presence pulling at him. Truthfully, he'd simply wanted to see Mattie Farrell.

So why was he hesitating? It wasn't like him to feel this unsure of himself around a woman. He started up the walk. If business wasn't a good enough excuse, it was certainly logical that he might drop by to see if she was all right. When he'd taken Joel's advice, he'd promised himself that he'd see to it Mattie wasn't hurt in any way by their partnership. And after this afternoon's discovery, he realized that even someone like Mac Delaney might pay her a visit. In fact, it was probably inevitable. The image of Mac having a cozy little chat with Mattie in the parlor was enough to quicken his step.

The music began as he climbed the porch stairs. It was a tinny-sounding piano playing a song that he couldn't place. Behind him, Hannibal whined. Even as he turned to see the dog collapse at the foot of the stairs, the front door opened.

When Mattie appeared a moment later, he frowned at her. "You're going to have to get the door fixed. It shouldn't swing open like that. I could be an ax murderer."

"In Barclayville?" She stepped back to let him in. "Besides, your great-aunt only plays this for you."

"Mendelssohn's Wedding March" rose to a crescendo in the dining room.

"It seems to be your theme song," she added.

The first thing Grant saw was the urn back in front of the staircase. "Why is she doing this?" he asked.

"She's getting to you. I knew it."

"It's a purely hypothetical question," he said.

Mattie shrugged. "I really don't know. My best guess is that she has something against stairs. There's a cold spot at the very top, but not everyone feels it. Lily shivers, but Ada Mae sails right through it every time. Maybe she's trying to discourage the guests from wandering up there." As she spoke, Mattie started to close the door. Hannibal whined. "Does he want to come in?"

"Once he heard the music, he decided to keep his distance."

Mattie turned to find Grant on his hands and knees running his hand over the floor near the stairs. "Seems level," he said as he stood up and pushed the urn under the banister.

"It is," Mattie said. "I checked it out first thing. C'mon." She led the way down the hall to the dining room. When she turned the lights on, the music stopped. "You can check to see if the harpsichord has an automatic player mechanism."

"A harpsichord." Grant moved toward it. "I wondered what it was."

"I found it in the attic."

For a moment, Grant said nothing. He was remembering a dream he'd had more than once as a child after his mother had died. There'd been music, faint and tinny-sounding. It had reminded him of a musical toy he'd had. And of his mother. It was a melody that she'd hummed often. When he turned to Mattie, he wasn't sure what to say.

She was smiling, but it was understanding, not laughter, he saw in her eyes. "There isn't a rational explanation for everything that goes on in this house," she said. "How about a beer?"

Grant followed her into the front parlor and settled himself on one of the sofas while she poured beer and a glass of wine for herself. When she handed him his drink, he set it on the table, careful not to disturb the papers she had spread out there. One had fallen on the floor. A list. Mattie Farrell was organized to a tee. His own approach to life was casual, some might say haphazard, but organization was a quality that he always admired. Suddenly, the words on her list began to register in his mind, and he picked it up to take a closer look. *Black Forest cake, family, friends, lovers.* Then an arrow pointing to *Grant Whittaker.*

Mattie knew exactly what was on the paper. She'd tossed it on the floor on purpose. It took every ounce of her control not to snatch it out of his hands. When he finally met her eyes, eyebrows raised, she wanted very badly to punch the grin off his face. "It's not what you think." Lame, lame, lame. How was she supposed to explain? She couldn't even rationalize to herself how she'd come to scribble his name after the word *lovers.* She'd been sitting in the very spot he was in now under the Whittaker family portrait when it had all come flooding back, every sensation that she'd experienced that morning when Hannibal had dug up the bones. The cold had been so sudden, so intense. Then she'd suddenly remembered how Grant had kissed her, how she'd kissed him back, and she'd stopped shivering.

Lifting her chin, she said, "Usually when I can't sleep, I work on menus. Tonight, that didn't work, so I started making a list of suspects." She took a sip of her wine and kept her attention fixed on Grant. She didn't want to think about the cellar again. "People who might have killed your great-aunt." So far, the grin hadn't faded from his face. "I read once that ninety-five percent of the time, people are murdered by someone close to them. Family."

Grant nodded helpfully. "Cain and Abel."

"Right." Her fingers tightened on her wineglass.

"But your family wasn't like that."

Mattie blinked. "No, of course not. Not that we didn't have some good fights. But we wouldn't actually—" Suddenly, she grinned. "Although I can remember one time that my sister, Peg, *wanted* to kill me. She was ten, and it was the very first time she made lasagne in my mom's restaurant. I burned it. Not on purpose. Still, I'm glad Peg wasn't a cop then. If she'd had a gun . . ." Mattie shook her head. "My mom, too. She wasn't pleased."

"You really have been in the restaurant business for a long time."

Mattie nodded. "I still work for my mother. She runs two places in Syracuse, so whenever I can, I try to stay there and help her out during the first part of the week."

"You were wrong." Setting her list on the table, Grant rose and walked toward her. "We aren't so very different, you and I. We both grew up in the kitchens of restaurants." He traced his finger along the lace collar of her blouse.

For a moment, Mattie didn't speak. She couldn't. He was close again. Just as close as he'd been in the cellar. She could recall each sensation she'd felt when he'd held her. And abruptly it occurred to her that if she closed the distance between them, she could experience it all again. The press of his fingers against the back of her neck, the heat of his breath on her skin, the quick whip of excitement that had spiraled through her. No one had ever made her feel like that before.

"You still haven't explained why you wrote the word *lovers* with an arrow pointing to my name," Grant said.

"It's simple," she said, even though what she was feeling wasn't. "In the middle of writing that list, I started thinking about what we were doing in the cellar just before Hannibal started to bark." Not for the life of her would she admit how quickly her coldness had vanished or how vivid the memory had been.

"You were thinking of death, and your mind took you back to life. A healthy progression."

To Mattie's surprise, the teasing look had completely disappeared from his eyes. She hadn't expected understanding. She found it more potent than his charm. And more dangerous.

Distance. That's what she needed. "Look." She moved behind the other sofa and began to pace. "I don't want to send off the wrong signals. I would be lying if I said that I didn't enjoy that kiss." She paused beneath the portrait. "But I meant what I said this afternoon. We're business associates. Expanding this place—" she waved a hand "—making it successful, it's a dream that I've had for a long time." She perched on the arm of the sofa. "I couldn't help overhearing the phone call you got in the diner yesterday," she added. "You seem to have a lot on your plate right now, too."

Her argument was cool, logical and one hundred percent on target. It occurred to him that Joel Lawson couldn't have made a better one. Getting custody of J.D. was his first priority. It had to be. But as he looked at Mattie sitting beneath the portrait of his great-aunt, he had a feeling, a premonition perhaps, that as much as they might each prefer it otherwise, they were going to make time, make "room" for each other. Before he could stop himself, he asked, "Have you ever heard of having your cake and eating it, too?"

"It depends on the cake," Mattie replied. "If it's blue, I'll pass." She set her glass down on the paper, right smack on top of his name. "I'm not interested in a one-night stand, a summer romance, a short-term affair or a relationship right now. Clear?"

"Perfectly." Grant raised his glass in a toast. To his great-aunt, to Mattie, perhaps both, and put it down on the word *lovers*. Then he sat down on the sofa opposite Mattie's and drew the partnership papers out of his pocket. "Business it is."

"For now."

Grant heard the words quite clearly. He knew he hadn't said them because they'd been spoken in a female voice. And Mattie's lips hadn't moved. He hadn't taken his eyes off her for a second. If she'd heard them, she wasn't giving any sign. Fine. He spread the partnership agreement open on the table. "My attorney drew up these documents when I was at his office yesterday. I'm offering you more than a lease. I'm prepared to make a sizable investment in the improvements that will be needed to get the Barclay mansion in shape. Everything you outlined this afternoon is fine, but I will need a small suite of rooms in the mansion so that I can move in there with my son." He flipped some pages and turned the document so that she could read it. "The figures are here, all based on your projections. You did a very impressive job. The money that I'm investing should allow the inn to be fully operational by this fall, all ten rooms." He pointed to a column of figures. "You won't have to wait for the first year's profits to complete the work on the third floor or finish the library."

When Mattie simply stared at him, saying nothing, Grant said, "If you're worried about the skeleton, don't be. I think that if word gets around outside of Barclayville, it will just add a certain mystique to the place." When he'd talked to Joel earlier this morning, he'd been more concerned about Lisa's reaction than about business, but his friend had been more amused than concerned. "My attorney says with a ghost and a skeleton, it's too bad we can't claim a pirate, too."

"No," Mattie said.

"He meant the pirate as a joke. I just wanted to set your mind at ease about the bones."

"I meant no to your offer. Thank you. But I can't accept."

It was Grant's turn to stare. "You can't be serious. It's very generous considering that I own both of the buildings." His eyes narrowed. "If that's what's worrying you, your profit margin the first year will allow you to exercise your option to buy Whittaker House. That way, we'll each own one of the buildings. That would keep the partnership on an equal footing."

"I don't want a partner. Ever. I had one once. It was a mistake, and I promised myself that I would never make it again."

Baffled, Grant rose. "This wouldn't be a mistake. I'm offering you exactly what you need, the cash to make your dream come true. You won't walk away from that."

"Watch me." She moved toward him, then said, "You lied to me, didn't you? 'Get out of Barclayville,' you told me. And all that concern about the curse? I almost believed you, and all along you were planning to stay here and open an inn." She poked a finger into his chest. "That's exactly what my partner did to me in Maryland. He liked my 'vision,' too, and he had money to invest. Then, as soon as the inn was operating at a profit, he showed me the clause in the contract that gave him the right to buy me out. I won't let you get away with that, and I'm not leaving Barclayville."

He grabbed her hand before she could poke him again for emphasis. As he did, the ring she wore caught the light. "That partner of yours, is he the one who gave you this?"

"No. Not that it's any—"

"Oh, it's my business, all right."

When he met her eyes, she felt her throat go completely dry. Beneath that easygoing exterior was a temper that threatened to leap right out and grab you. She'd never seen his eyes frost over quite that way before. But she was almost sure that it wasn't fear that had made her legs feel suddenly numb or her hand go suddenly limp in his.

"Because you and I are going to be partners. I want to see your plans for the Barclay mansion become a reality as much as you do." He realized it was true as he said the words. They were standing close, just as close as they'd been standing in the cellar that afternoon. "And nothing from the past, yours or mine, is going to stand in the way." That was true, too, he realized. And he would have denied both statements before he'd walked through the door of Whittaker House tonight. Though he didn't glance away from Mattie, Grant was aware of his great-aunt looking down on them from the portrait.

He released her hand and stepped back from her then. "Think about it." He wasn't sure whether he was talking to Mattie or himself. As he strode into the foyer, the front door swung open. He pretended to ignore it and the scent of lilacs as he walked down the porch steps.

MATTIE WOKE UP in the middle of the night. Groggy, she thought it was a dream that had awakened her. Grant Whittaker. And she'd just about convinced him to forget about his partnership offer and just sign her lease. Damn it! A few more minutes and she'd have had his signature on the dotted line. She rolled onto her back and tried to slip back into her dream. The ringing of the phone finally registered. Turning, she stared in the direction of the noise. Who could be calling at this hour?

Her family. Throwing the blanket back, she hurried across the small room, banged into the desk and felt for the phone. "Yes?"

"*Get out of Barclayville.*"

"Now, just a minute—" Mattie broke off when she realized that she was talking to a dial tone. Astonished, she stared at the receiver. Then she glanced down at the Call I.D. box that her mother had insisted she buy. But it was too late. The number had disappeared. Who?

Grant Whittaker! Fury rolled through her as she tossed off her nightshirt and pulled on jeans and a shirt. She made it to the door before it hit her.

The doubt. Grant wouldn't have done something like this. He couldn't possibly have thought that he could frighten her with a crank call. Could he? It hadn't been his voice. But it had sounded distorted as if it was a tape being played on a slow speed.

Turning, she began to pace. Besides, he didn't really want to scare her out of town. He wanted her to be his partner. Frowning, she whirled at the window and walked back to the door. Was that true or was it something she just wanted to believe?

Get out of Barclayville! He'd said those exact words to her in the diner that first day.

Think, Mattie. That's what her father would tell her. *Your head's better than your fists!* Grant claimed they needed each other to make the Whittaker Inn a reality. She certainly needed him because he owned the buildings. But did he really need her?

Mattie sat down on her cot and stared at the phone for a long time. Finally, she made her decision. She wouldn't tell him about the phone call. If he had made it, she wasn't going to give him the satisfaction of acknowledging it.

And if it hadn't been Grant? She was still considering that possibility when the sky outside the window was bright and the bird song loud.

4

THE FIRST SIGN of disaster was her Toyota pulling sharply to the left on the two-lane road. Then the noise shattered the Sunday-morning silence. *Whackety-whackety-whackety!* Gripping the steering wheel, Mattie wrestled the car onto the gravel shoulder, then sat scowling at the windshield.

She didn't have to look to know that another tire had blown. Two flats in less than a week. Lightning wasn't supposed to strike twice! A long roll of thunder rumbled ominously overhead.

She glanced up at the sky. There was no sign of rain. Yet. But there were times when everything that could go wrong did. That's what her life had been like ever since Grant Whittaker had walked out of Whittaker House on Friday night.

Not that she could blame everything on him. He definitely hadn't made the anonymous phone call. In the more rational light of day, she'd finally remembered that her Call I.D. box had a memory. And when she'd punched up the last call, only the words *Out Of Area* had popped up on the display. So the call hadn't been made locally. That was even more puzzling. A long-distance crank call?

Then other crises had pushed the call out of her mind. First, there was the emergency sugar shortage that had forced her to drive on her spare tire. She couldn't lay that at Grant's door, either. But it *was* his great-aunt who had caused it.

On Saturday night, every single saltshaker had contained sugar. Ada Mae had insisted on tossing all of it, claiming that

Mattie Whittaker couldn't be trusted not to have contaminated the sugar with salt.

Then there was the house itself. It had seemed so quiet after the last guests had left. No music, no scent of lilacs. Even the urn had stayed put. Mattie had thought long and hard about it as she paced in the front parlor. Could it be that Mattie Whittaker was upset by the discovery of her skeleton after all these years?

Twice, she'd found herself reaching for the phone to call Grant. He hadn't stopped by, not that she'd expected him to. After all, she'd made her position quite clear. Refusing his partnership offer had been the right decision. She certainly couldn't blame him for taking her at her word. She should have been relieved that he'd been so easy to convince.

So why wasn't she? With a shake of her head, Mattie glanced at her watch. Twelve-thirty. She didn't have time to worry about Grant Whittaker. It was Sunday and her first reservations were at four o'clock. She'd just put Grant out of her mind. Grabbing the bag of sugar and the quart of blueberries, she crawled across the passenger seat, thinking it was going to be difficult to keep her mind off Grant while she was experimenting with a blueberry buckle recipe.

Whittaker House was just over the hill, so she didn't have far to walk. The day seemed to be looking up, when she heard the motorcycle approaching.

Grant Whittaker. Mattie knew it was him even before she turned around. She was not, absolutely *not*, pleased to see him. But as she watched him pull the bike to a stop and dismount, she couldn't help thinking that he looked like a knight of old riding in on his charger.

"Problem?" he asked, removing his helmet and getting off his motorcycle.

"Just a flat tire," Mattie said. "I'll fix it later."

His gaze fell on the blueberries and he grinned. "Don't tell me. You've developed a craving for blueberry buckle. I'm going to convert you to diner food yet."

"Don't get your hopes up. I'm planning on using these to convince you that a better presentation will only improve taste."

"We can settle that right now," Grant said. And then in a move so quick she couldn't avoid it, he cupped her chin with his hand and kissed her.

Only for a moment, Grant promised himself. He hadn't thought of anything but her since he'd left Whittaker House on Friday night. He'd stayed away as part of his strategy for dealing with her. And then the moment he'd seen her, he'd wanted to kiss her.

When her lips warmed and parted and he sampled her taste, it was sweeter than he remembered. So he took another moment. He felt her breath mingle with his and her pulse begin to throb where his fingers rested beneath her jaw.

He wanted to touch her, too. More than anything, he wanted to slip his hands beneath that white T-shirt and feel the heat of her skin.

He wanted. Perhaps more than he'd ever wanted before. It might have been that realization that made him release her and step back.

Cautious wasn't a word he'd often applied to himself before. This was a new experience.

Mattie stared at him as he drew away and tried to hold on to the packages she was carrying. She'd almost dropped them, she'd wanted to touch him so much. His kiss had been soft and it hadn't lasted very long, but for a moment she'd felt such pleasure, such greed.

"You win," he said, interrupting her thoughts. "The presentation was terrific, the taste even better. Give me your keys. I'll get the spare out." He smiled and held out his hand.

"There is no spare."

He chuckled. "Sure there is. It's just tucked away in the well." He circled around the passenger side, then turned back to her with a frown. "You're already driving on the spare."

Chin in the air, she told him, "I had a flat on the way to meet you Thursday. That's why I was late."

"And you haven't taken care of it yet?"

"I've been busy."

"Too busy to take care of your own personal safety?" He shot a look at her as he bent over to examine the flat. "This tire's bald." Even as he spoke, he was up and walking around the car, checking the other tires. "They're *all* bald. Do you have a death wish?"

He stopped in front of her and Mattie saw the accusation in his eyes. The fact that he was right embarrassed her. "I know I need new tires. It's on one of my lists."

"Time to cross it off," Grant said. "My mother was killed in a car accident. I believe strongly in taking reasonable precautions. Bob Bailey runs a service station in Mason's Corners." He lifted her hand to look at her watch and frowned. "He's gone fishing by now. I have business in Albany or I'd take a shot at finding him and drag him back to the station." Pulling her by the wrist, he said, "I'll give you a lift home."

"I'm perfectly capable of—"

"Taking care of yourself?" Grant took the blueberries and sugar from her and packed them in the compartment on the back of the bike. "With two flats in less than a week?" He unhooked the spare helmet and placed it on her head. "Get on. I have an appointment in Albany in an hour. I'll drop you off."

Mattie didn't argue. Gingerly, she placed her arms around him, closed her eyes and offered up a prayer of thanks that the ride over the hill was so short. Too short to worry about falling off. Too short to think about her body pressed against his. And much too short to think about the kiss he'd given her. Or the one she'd given him back.

The moment he stopped the bike in front of Whittaker House, she jumped off, handed him the helmet and started up the driveway.

"Mattie?"

She turned.

"Don't you want your blueberries?"

MATTIE FROWNED as she watched him drive off. His parting words had been, "I'll be back tomorrow. Save me a taste." What kind of business would keep Grant Whittaker in Albany overnight? The worrisome question was forgotten the moment she spotted the back end of her mother's red Miata at the edge of the house. Immediately, her thoughts flew to her brother and sister-in-law who were expecting their first baby by the end of the summer. She broke into a run across the front lawn.

She heard the harpsichord before she reached the porch steps, and the door swung open.

She's feeling better! Mattie thought, relieved. As she entered the foyer, Mattie saw her mother step into the hallway carrying a tray. "That's a neat trick," her mother said, "opening the door that way! How on earth do you do it?"

Mattie set the sugar and blueberries on the floor before she closed the door firmly behind her. "Believe me, you don't want to know. Is C.J. all right?"

"She's fine." Carefully balancing the tray, her mother leaned over to inspect the door hinges. "Roarke's fine, your sister's fine and I'm fine. But I'll be much better after you tell me how you get this door to open automatically. And the music! I can't figure out how you do that either."

Her mother led the way into the parlor, saying, "At first, I thought it was a recording, but while I was making tea, I kept checking, and the keys work just as if an invisible person were sitting there, like one of those old player pianos." She poured Mattie a cup of tea. "I'd love to be able to do something like that at the Greenhouse. Would you mind? Not the door, of course. In the city, I couldn't have the door swinging open at all hours. You're lucky to be out here in the country where it's safe."

Mattie hid a smile behind her cup. There was no one quite like her mother. Gina Farrell had spent her life trying to make her children strong and independent, so there would be no lecture about the fact that she had been able to walk right into her daughter's empty restaurant and make a pot of tea. But neither would Gina let it slide. Just as she wouldn't let her questions about the door and the music go unanswered.

Sipping her tea, Mattie considered her options. Lying was definitely out. Her mother had a built-in lie detector that never failed. Changing the subject would offer only a slight reprieve. Mattie knew the small dark-haired woman sitting across from her very well. At fifty-five, Gina Farrell had the energy of a woman half her age, and she was tenacious when she set her mind on something. Mattie took another quick sip of her tea and decided to save herself some time. "Whittaker House has a ghost who smells like lilacs, plays the harpsichord and opens the front door when she's in the mood."

Gina's eyebrows shot up. "A ghost?"

Mattie pointed to the portrait above the mantel. "That's her in the picture. The young girl."

Gina rose to look more closely. "Pretty." Then she turned to her daughter. "Your restaurant is haunted."

It was a statement. Apparently, her mother's built-in lie detector was still in perfect operating condition.

"Tell me more," Gina said.

"She used to run a boardinghouse here, she was an excellent cook and she has an interesting sense of humor. Last

night, for instance, she put sugar in all the saltshakers."
Mattie waved a hand. "That's part of her regular routine, but
last night she switched the canisters, too, and I very nearly
put salt in my chocolate mousse."

Gina laughed, then threw her daughter an apologetic look.
"Not funny, I know. How did she manage that?"

"I was distracted." That much was true. She'd been thinking about Grant Whittaker and his partnership offer.

Gina sat down. "Because of the skeleton business."

Mattie's tea sloshed over the rim of her cup.

Gina smiled at Mattie's stunned expression. "Your brother
has friends everywhere. Someone in the state police recognized the name Farrell and gave him a call. He was going to
pay you a visit, but I told him that I was dying to take the
Miata out for a spin. Such a lovely day to ride with the top
down. Until I got near Barclayville. There seems to be a big
black cloud over this town today."

"Every day," Mattie muttered as she blotted up the tea with
her napkin.

Gina tucked her legs beneath her. "I want to know all about
the bones in the Barclay mansion. That way, I can keep
Roarke from descending on you. C.J. needs him right now."

It wasn't an idle threat. Mattie knew she'd be facing her
brother right now if Gina hadn't intervened, so she poured
out the story of Mattie Whittaker, the curse, Hannibal's discovery of the bones, layering on the details but leaving out
the threatening phone call. When she finished, Gina was
looking at the portrait. "Such a tragedy. She was so young."

Mattie nodded, and for a moment her mother's eyes met
hers as they both remembered another untimely death. Rising, Gina moved to sit next to her daughter and took her
hand. "This must have been very hard for you." Mattie had
been closest to her father; she'd even refused to cry at the fu-
neral. She squeezed Mattie's hand before releasing it. "Maybe

she'll finally be able to rest once you go ahead with your plans to expand your inn."

"*If* I go ahead."

"I assumed from what you said that Mr. Whittaker had agreed to cooperate."

Mattie started to reach for her cup, then feeling the need to move, rose and walked behind the opposite sofa. "He wants to be my partner." She began to pace. "Of course, I told him it was out of the question, that I'd had a partner once. Never again!" She whirled to face her mother. "I'd be a fool to trust anyone like that again, wouldn't I?"

Gina leaned back against the cushions and studied her daughter. "That depends. You can always have your brother or C.J. check the partnership agreement and tie everything up legally to make sure that it works to your advantage this time."

"Yeah." Mattie straightened the protective cover on the arm of the sofa, then perched on it.

"But it isn't the legal aspect that has you worried, is it?" Gina reached for her cup and took a sip. "Are you attracted to Grant Whittaker?"

Mattie sprang up and began to pace again. "I just hate to make the same mistake twice!"

Gina's eyebrows rose. "Speaking for myself, I've never liked making a mistake the first time."

With a sudden laugh, Mattie sat down next to her. "Mom, there is absolutely no one like you."

"That's because God doesn't like to repeat his mistakes, either." Gina gave her daughter a quick hug. "So what do you want to do?"

Mattie sighed. "I want to turn this place into the best country inn in upstate New York." She glanced at the portrait. "And I want to find out what happened to Mattie Whittaker."

"And Mr. Whittaker's partnership offer is attractive?"

Very attractive, Mattie thought, and wished it were only the offer she found so appealing. "He plans to invest enough money to make the place fully operational by the fall. By myself, I'd need at least two years and a lot of reservations."

Gina nodded. "A very tempting offer. But risky."

"Maybe even riskier if I don't take it." Mattie frowned. "When he dropped me off just now, he was on his way to Albany for a business meeting. He's on the faculty of the hotel management school at Cornell. He could redo the mansion and open up in competition with me. If he tries it . . ."

"You could always move to a new town," Gina said. "In this area, of course, where your reputation is established."

Mattie rose, walked a few steps, then stopped. There was no place else she wanted to be. "No. I don't want to leave. I can't. Something, someone, maybe Mattie Whittaker, drew me to this place." She turned to the portrait. "Of course, I researched the location and discovered that it had potential, but from the very first day, I felt like I was meant to be here." She gave her mother an exasperated look and sat down on the arm of the couch. "I know what it sounds like. A ghost brought me here! Crazy! But someone has to find out what really happened. All these years, people have believed they were living under a curse."

"It won't bring her back," Gina said.

"But maybe it will bring her some peace." Mattie drew in a deep breath and folded her hands on her lap. "Besides, I won't run away. Not again."

Rising, Gina walked to Mattie and took her hands. "If you don't want to run, you have two options. You can stay and fight."

Mattie's fingers curled tightly around her mother's. "Careful, you sound just like Dad."

Gina rolled her eyes. "Heaven forbid. I'm not suggesting that you give the poor man a black eye. In fact, the second option is always preferable—compromise."

Mattie wrinkled her nose as she walked with her mother into the foyer.

"I'll tell Roarke not to worry," Gina said. "Tempest in a teapot. After all, what kind of danger could there be? After fifty years, whoever killed her is probably dead."

Mattie thought fleetingly of the anonymous phone call and kept her smile firmly in place.

"And you're not to think of commuting back and forth to Syracuse at the beginning of the week anymore," Gina said. "I can manage at the Greenhouse. You stay here until your business with Mr. Whittaker is settled."

"You're sure you don't need me?" Mattie asked.

"We discussed all this before. Once you start the renovations, you'll have to be here all the time anyway." Gina hugged Maggie as strains of Mendelssohn floated down the hallway.

GRANT PACED in the suite of rooms his ex-mother-in-law had assigned to him. The summons to Albany for dinner had been the last thing he'd needed. Lisa's doctors would not permit her to make a transcontinental trip, and so Lisa's mother had volunteered for the job of checking out Grant's living arrangements. Just one more hoop to jump through. He would have been sorely tempted to refuse, in spite of his attorney's advice, if it hadn't been for the news that J.D. was visiting his grandmother. He couldn't pass up an opportunity to be with his son.

Running his hands through his hair, he sat on the side of the bed. Seeing J.D. had been the only worthwhile thing about the trip. Dinner had been accompanied by an in-depth interrogation about his plans for providing a suitable home environment for his son.

He'd had to dance around the issue of his partnership agreement with the stubborn Ms. Farrell. At some point on the motorcycle ride to Albany, he'd decided that with a little time, Mattie would see the wisdom of his offer. After all, she was an organized, list-making businesswoman. Eventually, she would be won over by the bottom line. He got up and started to pace again. If he could just keep himself from pressuring her, she'd see the logic of signing the agreement.

Unfortunately, he'd lost count of the times he'd had to stop himself from picking up the phone or taking Hannibal for a walk past Whittaker House. Just as he'd lost count of the times he'd thought of her. And when he'd met her this morning on the side of the road... Well, he'd managed not to bring up the partnership, but then his mind hadn't been on business.

The woman had gotten under his skin, and he wasn't even sure why. Where was it going to lead? She'd made it crystal clear she didn't want a personal relationship. And he certainly didn't need one. Not when he had J.D. to think about.

Still, he couldn't rid his thoughts of Mattie Farrell. She was alone in that house. He remembered Mac Delaney's words about there not being a statute of limitations on murder. If he weren't in Albany, he could take Hannibal and walk by just to check on her.

He reached for the phone and punched in the number of Whittaker House. It rang four times before he heard her voice.

"Whittaker House. If you'd like to—"

"Mattie—" He stopped when he realized that he was talking to a machine. He glanced at his watch. Midnight. Surely she was there. Impatient, he waited for the tone. "Mattie, are you there?"

"Grant?" She sounded out of breath.

"Are you all right?"

He sounded concerned, wonderful. "Fine. I was washing my hair and I had to run." She felt foolish for the panic she'd felt when she'd first heard the phone. Cowardly, in fact, because she hadn't picked it up when she'd seen Out of Area on the Call I.D. box display. "Is there a problem?" she asked.

"Several." Not the least of which was that he was wondering what her hair would look like wet, and what the weight of it would feel like in his hand. "Look. I got in touch with Bob Bailey, the service-station guy I told you about. He's going to tow your car in, first thing in the morning."

"And you called at midnight to tell me that?" She leaned against the edge of her desk, trying to ignore her own pleasure at the idea.

"Not just that. I couldn't wait until tomorrow to find out how the blueberry buckle turned out."

Mattie responded to the grin in his voice. "Aha! I've got you worried."

"Who me? Not a bit. You'll never figure out George's secret ingredient."

There was a loud rumble of thunder, and Mattie watched the lights flicker.

"What's going on?" Grant asked.

"Just a storm. It's been raining off and on all day."

There was a tap at his door. J.D. appeared and Grant motioned the little boy in. "Mattie, I can't talk now. Do you have Delaney's phone number?"

"He's in the book, isn't he?"

"Look it up and write down the number. I have to go, and I won't be back until tomorrow morning. Promise me you'll call him if there's any trouble."

"What kind of—" There was another loud crack of thunder, and Mattie found herself talking to a dial tone. She used a little extra force to settle the receiver back in its cradle, then she began to pace.

What kind of trouble did he expect? When the towel slipped from her hair and fell onto her bare feet, she kicked it out of the way. And what kind of business did he have in Albany? Had he taken her answer as final and decided to find himself a new business partner?

She grabbed the towel and began to dry her hair. Grant Whittaker was an annoying, distracting, attractive and maddening man. If he were here right now—

Outside, there was a clap of thunder, followed by the hiss and crackle of lightning, and the lights went out. Mattie whirled and bumped her hip against the doorknob on her way out of the room.

The candles were all downstairs, and Ada Mae kept matches in the kitchen. She was at the head of the stairs when she heard the noise.

A board creaking. On the porch? She heard it again. Thunder exploded overhead, and for a second lightning illuminated the foyer. She strained to listen. Nothing. Minutes ticked by, but all she heard was the sound of her own breathing. Finally, she pushed herself away from the wall. Grant's talk about trouble and the electrical storm had spooked her, that was all. Old houses made all kinds of strange noises.

She lowered her foot to the first step, and the cold hit her with the force of a truck. Her hand went numb on the railing, her face froze. She couldn't even blink. For one frightening second, she thought she was paralyzed, and then suddenly she broke free and stumbled back two steps until she was flat against the wall. Wrapping her arms around herself to keep from shaking, she waited, barely breathing. Gradually her eyes adjusted to the darkness; she could distinguish darker and lighter patches. When she squinted, she could even make out the shape of the banister and front door.

Thunder rumbled again, farther away, on a long echoing roll. As it faded, she heard the soft scrape of metal rubbing against metal. That wasn't something she could blame on the house. Even as she swallowed the rising bubble of panic, she pictured clearly in her mind the front doorknob turning slowly. She didn't breathe, she couldn't while her heart was beating like a bird's wings in her throat.

It seemed like forever until she heard the sound of wood meeting resistance. The lock had held. Her relief was short-lived; she thought of the back door with its panel of glass. And there were windows.

No. Pushing back the wave of hysteria, she forced herself to take a deep, calming breath. And she smelled lilacs.

She wasn't alone.

Another sound floated up the stairs, whispery soft. Mattie couldn't quite place it. Another board creaked. The bottom porch step? Then nothing. She waited, counting the seconds as they passed; even the thunder had stopped. When she got to twenty, she heard the muffled sound of an engine. Hurrying to the front bedroom, she was in time to the see the headlights of a car disappearing over the hill.

Her mind was racing as she carefully made her way down the stairs. In the kitchen, she located Ada Mae's store of matches and picked up the candle on the first table she came to in the dining room.

There wasn't a doubt in her mind that whoever had tried to get in the front door was gone, but would the intruder return? The question might be easier to answer if she could figure out what had brought the person to Whittaker House in the first place.

She saw the square of paper a second before she stepped on it. It was just inside the foyer, touching the urn. She crouched over, lowering the candle, and black letters cut from newspaper headlines jumped out at her.

LEAVE BARCLAYVILLE.

Oddly, the words didn't scare her. Instead, she felt the beginning of anger. Good. She was tired of being frightened, and anger would help her think. Lifting the note by its corner, she carried it into the parlor and set it along with the candle, on the table beneath the fireplace. The flame sent a flickering play of light and shadows along the walls of the room.

Someone wanted her out of Barclayville. Mattie sank onto the nearest sofa and folded her hands in her lap as she began to sift and sort through the possibilities. She'd had Whittaker House open a year, and no one had been bothered in the least. No, it was the Barclay mansion that had somebody all worked up. Lifting her candle, she rose and turned to face the portrait. "I'm staying. And I'm going to find out how you died." It was only a trick of light, she was sure, but Mattie could have sworn that the girl in the portrait smiled at her.

THE SUN WAS BEATING DOWN, turning the previous night's rainfall into a steam bath. Mattie walked into the parking lot of George's Diner, shifting the basket she was carrying to her other arm and reaching behind to unstick her damp shirt from her back. She frowned at the silver Mercedes parked chummily next to Grant Whittaker's black motorcycle. It was the same Mercedes that she'd seen follow Grant's motorcycle to the Barclay mansion an hour and a half ago.

She'd been in the parlor debating whether or not to take the batch of blueberry buckle she'd just pulled from the oven to the diner. Not as a peace offering, certainly. And not even under pain of torture would she ever admit that her first batch had been the pale blue color of a baby's bunting, nor that she'd finally had to poke the berries into the batter by hand to achieve the results she wanted.

Then she'd heard the roar of Grant's motorcycle, and thought the decision had been taken from her. By the time she'd reached the window, though, Grant had whipped past Whittaker House and taken a left up the hill leading to the Barclay mansion. A silver Mercedes with a blonde behind the wheel was close behind.

The first thought that popped into Mattie's mind was that at least the woman wasn't sitting behind him on the bike, plastered to his back. She was appalled.

Mattie took a hanky out of her pocket and wiped the back of her neck. Jealousy was impossible. Any discomfort she experienced because of a blond woman in the Mercedes was strictly on a professional level. After all, hadn't Grant said that he was in Albany on business? It was entirely possible that this person was a prospective business partner. And Mattie intended to take care of that right now. Sometime in the middle of a sleepless night, she'd decided that accepting Grant's offer was the logical thing to do. This time, she would simply follow her head, not her heart. And to make sure of that, she'd added a few terms to the partnership agreement. The list was in her pocket.

She was halfway to the steps when she heard Hannibal's bark and a child's voice. Even then she might have continued to the front door if she hadn't heard a trace of fear in the tone. She quickly detoured to the back of the diner.

A little boy stood on the grass neatly dressed in navy blue shorts, a T-shirt and matching vest. His small body was rigid, his hands clenched into fists. Hannibal sat directly in the child's path. Even seated, Hannibal was the taller of the two. The dog nudged a stick with his nose and barked.

"He wants you to throw it," Mattie said.

The little boy glanced at her through the wire-rimmed glasses perched on the tip of his nose. Eagerly, he picked up the stick and tossed it. Hannibal lumbered to his feet and loped off after it in slow motion.

"Hi, I'm Mattie Farrell."

The boy pushed his glasses up higher on his nose and gave her a solemn look. "I'm not supposed to talk to strangers."

Mattie squatted so her eyes were level with his. "That's a good rule. But I'm not exactly a stranger. I know Mr. Whittaker, the man who runs the diner. In fact, I just dropped by to give him some blueberry buckle." She lifted the napkin in the basket so that the boy could take a peek. "And I know Hannibal here," she added as the dog skidded into her leg and spit a soggy-looking stick in the boy's direction.

"He brought it back." The child grinned and this time when he picked up the stick, he put more energy into the pitch.

"Do you have a dog?" Mattie asked as they watched Hannibal lumber off.

"Two," he replied. "But they're Dobermans. I can't play with them." He studied Mattie for a moment. "Sometimes I sneak them something to eat." When she didn't reply, he continued, "I'm J.D. Whittaker. That's my dad's motorcycle over there. I get to ride on it sometimes."

"Really?"

He nodded, shot a quick look at the diner, then lowered his voice. "Not today because my grandmother's here. She's talking to my dad. She's scared of motorcycles. Snakes scare her, too. She screamed when I dropped one on her kitchen floor."

Mattie bit down on the inside of her cheek, to prevent grinning at the familiar gleam of mischief in J.D.'s eyes. "When I was five," she said, "I dropped a snake on my mother's bed, and she fainted."

The statement won her an admiring glance from J.D. A moment later, Hannibal came to a skidding halt next to them. "What did he do with the stick?" J.D. asked.

"He's sitting on it," she replied, "and I think he's going to take a nap. You know, there's a stream down that path. Would you like to go wading?"

J.D. shot her a grin. "Yeah."

Mattie began to have second thoughts about her suggestion the moment J.D. raced down the path. Her doubts only increased when they walked into the water and he stumbled. She didn't want to imagine his grandmother's reaction if he fell in. Tightening her grip on his hand, she led him onto a large flat rock where the water was only ankle-deep.

"Look," J.D. pointed at the shore. "Hannibal followed us." Then cupping his hands, he scooped up water and tossed it at the dog. He hit his target dead-on, but Hannibal didn't move a muscle. The boy gave Mattie a side-long glance.

"Don't even think about splashing me," she warned. "Unless you can hold your breath for a very long time."

J.D. grinned and said, "I can hold my breath for almost two minutes."

"But your clothes would get all wet. And you'd have mud all over your face and in your hair. I don't think your grandmother would like that."

His grin widened. "She'd be livid!"

"*Livid?* I'm impressed. That's a very good word. Do you know what it means?"

"Beet-red," he replied. "Grandmother caught me jumping up and down on my bed, and she said, 'That's a priceless antique! You're making me livid!' Her face got really red."

"I'll bet it did."

J.D. cupped some water in his hands, then spread his fingers and let it slip through. "What does security mean?"

Mattie thought for a minute. "I think it means having someone to give you hugs and tuck you under the covers at night." *Having someone to tow your car for you.* Where had that come from? She hoped she hadn't said it out loud. It wouldn't make sense to J.D. It didn't make any sense to her.

J.D. wrinkled his nose. "Really? Grandmother says it means a comfortable house, proper schools and maybe a nanny. She and my dad were talking about it."

"*Security* is one of those words that means different things to different people," Mattie said.

J.D. let another handful of water slide through his fingers. "Mom says I have to have it if I come to live with my dad."

"I see." Hannibal's head was up again. Mattie glanced at the basket of blueberry buckle a few yards away on the bank. "What did you think of that big old house?" she asked.

"Great place to play hide-and-seek!" J.D. sent a water missile at the dog. Hannibal rose slowly to his feet to shake himself. Mattie eyed her basket warily.

J.D. scooped up more water. "I don't think my grandmother liked it much. And then my dad started talking about a partner. That's when I got bored and hid in this little room. It took them a long time to find me."

Mattie might have laughed at the satisfaction in J.D.'s tone had she not pictured Grant and his ex-mother-in-law huddled together in the diner talking about a partnership.

Suddenly, J.D. burst into laughter. "Look at him run!"

Mattie whirled in time to see Hannibal racing away with her wicker basket clamped firmly between his jaws. She saw Grant on the path that led to the diner and yelled, "Stop him!" Grabbing J.D.'s hand, she started toward shore.

She stumbled and almost fell. If she took J.D. with her, she could just picture Grant's new partner turning livid!

Grant hadn't bothered to stop the dog. He was waiting for them on the shore, surprise and something else in his expression.

"I didn't expect to see you today," he said, helping them to solid ground.

"Mattie brought you some blueberry buckle," J.D. said. "But the dog stole it!"

Mattie frowned. "I wasted three hours making it." Then she could have bitten her tongue out for admitting it.

"Three hours?"

Laughter filled his eyes. "I'd be glad to give you some lessons in preparing diner food," he said. "It takes me about fifteen minutes." He lifted his son and settled the boy on his shoulders.

"Hers isn't blue," J.D. said. "His is the best!" he added to Mattie in a confidential tone.

Overhearing, Grant said, "Two against one. Maybe Hannibal will agree, and you can salvage some of your efforts."

He joined her in laughter and when their eyes met, and held for a moment, she felt a jolt right down to her toes. How could a moment of shared laughter possibly feel as intimate as the two kisses they'd shared? And why was she actually keeping count? Somewhere in the back of her mind, a warning voice cried loud and clear—*Run!*

She was almost sure that she was going to regret not heeding it.

"I've got to get J.D. back to the diner," Grant said. "His grandmother has a tennis lesson later this afternoon."

"Wait." Mattie gathered up J.D.'s socks and shoes, and followed them to the diner, where a petite blonde stood waiting next to the silver Mercedes. She was about the same age as Gina, Mattie guessed, and her tan had to have come out of a salon. The white tennis outfit set off the color perfectly. As she moved closer, Mattie expected to see aloofness in the woman's eyes. What she saw was worry.

"Mattie Farrell, I'd like you to meet my ex-mother-in-law, Lynda Ackerman."

As Mattie shook the older woman's hand, Lynda said, "Grant tells me that you're going to be his partner in this new inn he's opening."

"I am—" Only the pressure of Grant's foot on hers kept her from making the statement a question and in the same moment Mattie recognized two distinct feelings: relief that Grant hadn't decided to go into partnership with Lynda Ackerman, and annoyance that he'd just assumed she'd accept his offer. For now, she pushed both emotions aside.

"I was telling Lynda all about your plans for the expansion," he said.

Mattie managed a smile. "What did you think of the Barclay mansion?"

"I just hope the two of you haven't bitten off more than you can chew. Of course, Grant has filled me in on your experience, and while I'm relieved to know he'll have a partner with your expertise . . ." Her voice trailed off as she glanced at her grandson.

"You still have some reservations. I can certainly understand. It's going to take a lot of work. But I do think it's an absolute disgrace that a wonderful old home like the Barclay mansion has been allowed to sit empty for so many years. But it's got great potential, don't you think, furnished again with the proper antiques? You wouldn't happen to know of someone who could help us find the right pieces?"

Lynda looked at Grant. "You didn't mention anything about antiques."

"My partner's handling all that."

Lynda gave Mattie a thoughtful look. "I might be able to suggest some dealers. What are your plans for the master suite?"

"I'd like it to be as authentic as possible. But furniture isn't my thing, really." Mattie shrugged. "I'm basically a chef. Maybe you could come to Whittaker House for dinner. It would have to be on the weekend. We're only open Thursday through Sunday until we can expand. How far are you?"

"About an hour."

"So close? If you came Sunday afternoon, we could look around, and maybe you could get a better feel for the place. I'd love to know what you think of the restaurant. You and J.D. could have dinner and still be home before dark."

Lynda studied Mattie for a moment, then nodded. "Yes. I'll see you next Sunday, Ms. Farrell."

"Me, too," J.D. said.

"You, too, Twerp." Grant swung his son off his shoulders and settled him in the passenger seat of the Mercedes.

When the car had disappeared up the highway, he turned to Mattie. "She wasn't a happy camper until you brought up antiques. How can I thank you?"

"By leveling with me," Mattie said.

5

ARMED WITH two glasses of ice coffee, Grant walked around the counter and climbed onto a stool next to Mattie. She hadn't said a word since he'd escorted her into the diner, and neither had he. The only sound was the thrumming of the air conditioner, which was fighting a losing battle with the afternoon sun that poured through the windows.

Fixing drinks had given Grant some time. He'd wanted to tell her the truth from the beginning, so why was he hesitating now? Could it be he was afraid she'd turn down his partnership offer and walk away?

He set down the glass in front of her. She didn't reach for it, she didn't even glance up. Her hands were gripped tightly together on the counter, belying her cool and collected posture. He raised his glass in a toast. "Shall we drink to our new partnership?"

She turned to him then. "You were pretty confident that I'd change my mind, weren't you?"

"Haven't you?"

"I'll let you know. First, I want the truth. On Thursday, you refused to sign my lease. Then you suddenly want to become my partner. Why?"

Grant put down his glass, turned the stool so he faced her and confessed. "I have a chance to get custody of my son if I can convince my ex-wife that I can settle down and provide a secure environment for him. Translated, my attorney says that means I have to give up my consulting work for the university, at least temporarily. He also advised me to move into one of the houses I own in Barclayville and buy into a business. I had your two-year expansion plan for the Whittaker Inn in my pocket at the time." He met her eyes squarely. "I'd do anything—even risk the Whittaker Curse, if it exists—to get custody of J.D."

Mattie studied him for a moment. She'd asked him to level with her, hadn't she? She might as well hear it all. "You implied that giving up your consulting work might be temporary. Will our partnership be a temporary arrangement too?"

"I'm not sure." As he said the words, Grant realized they were true. And as short a time ago as last Thursday, he would have answered her question with an unqualified yes. Was he actually considering the possibility of remaining in Barclayville? He took a sip of his ice coffee, then turned back to Mattie. "Now it's your turn to level. Why did you change your mind about becoming my partner?"

With one finger, Mattie traced a line in the frost that had formed on her glass. "Ever since I was a little girl, I've wanted to run an inn in the country. My father used to talk about doing it all the time. After my experience in Maryland, I'm not too keen on having a partner." She turned to meet Grant's eyes. "But the bottom line is that I think we both have a lot to gain from what you're offering." *And everything to lose.* The thought slipped into her mind, but she ignored it. After all, Grant hadn't told her anything that she hadn't been fully prepared for. Unzipping the pouch she wore around her waist, she pulled out a piece of paper and handed it to him. "I do have some things I'd like clearly spelled out in the agreement."

Grant looked at the list, precisely printed, neatly numbered, and he began to relax. He saw that Mattie was tense, waiting. He relaxed even more, leaning his elbow on the counter and began to read aloud. "Number one—you are the only person who can buy me out. And what if I don't like the terms?"

"I'm sure I can meet any fair terms you'd request. The problem is that I'd need time. We can have the lawyers figure out the language so that we're both protected. But I'm not in a position right now to go into a bidding war with someone like your ex-mother-in-law, for example."

Grant's eyebrows rose. "You think she'd like to get involved?"

"I think I might have opened a can of worms asking her advice about antiques."

Grant shook his head. "Lynda has a very busy schedule at the country club. But J.D. means a lot to her. And you very cleverly pointed out that if she can approve of this new custody arrangement, she'll be able to see him a lot more often than she did while he was living with Lisa in California. I still don't know how to thank you for that."

"You've already done that by being honest. So how about it? Can we let the lawyers have their fun putting number one into the agreement?"

"Absolutely. Have you got a pen?"

She dug one out of her pouch, and he used it to check off the first item on her list. "Let's see—number two, you have the final word on food."

"Read that to mean no blue cake."

"In spite of J.D.'s endorsement?"

"You can always whip up a batch just for him and serve it in the diner."

"Okay, I can live with that, until I can get you to change your mind." He made another check on the paper. "Number three—our relationship will be strictly business."

Glancing at Mattie, he let himself recall how he'd felt down at the stream when he'd seen her with his son. The sunlight had been pouring over her then, in much the same way it was now, emphasizing the red highlights in her hair. They'd been talking and laughing, and for a moment, his mind had been wiped completely clean, to be filled up with a longing so deep he ached. He hadn't wanted to think about what he was feeling then, and he didn't want to think about it now. But he knew that all the lawyers in the world couldn't figure out a way to protect them from what was going to happen, what was already happening between them. Without a word, he placed a check by number three.

Mattie let out the breath she'd been holding. She certainly hadn't expected it to be that easy. When he reached out to grip her chin, she knew she'd been right.

"I suppose you think our lives are complicated enough," he said. "And that since our business arrangement may be only temporary, we're both smart enough—levelheaded enough—to see that any kind of personal relationship would only interfere with productivity, or the bottom line. Right?"

His voice was calm, but his eyes weren't. They had darkened like a summer sky before a storm, and they held a promise of pleasure. She could almost feel his touch on her skin, the liquid fire that would engulf her. All she had to do was lean a little closer and his lips would be on hers. It was just a matter of inches. She felt as if she was being pulled by a force as natural and as inexorable as gravity. And he knew it. She could see it in his eyes, in the curve of his mouth. He was waiting, watching her, willing her to make that move ... so he could cross out number three from their agreement. Mattie stiffened her spine and stayed perfectly still. "Absolutely right," she said.

He grinned at her and released her chin. "Fine! But I've made my point. You wanted to kiss me just now, as much as I wanted to kiss you."

Mattie lifted her chin. "We don't always get what we want."

"In this case we will," he argued. "Strictly business. You can have your attorneys write it into the agreement any way they want, and we can both sign on the dotted line." He leaned closer to her. "But nothing—not one thing we put in writing or swear to each other—is going to change what's going to happen between us. Because we're already personally involved, and that involvement is going to get very intimate."

Mattie was so intent on Grant, so riveted by what he was saying, she didn't realize he was taking her hand in his.

"Who gave you this ring?" he asked, raising their joined hands. The stone sent prisms of light dancing over the countertops and across the walls of the diner.

"My father gave it to me for my tenth birthday. It was his last gift to me." She leaned forward and spoke in a very soft voice. "It's no one's business but mine whose ring I wear. And as far as our relationship goes—" she leaned even closer "—it will only get as personal or as intimate as I want."

Grant's laugh erupted, quick and easy. He placed her hand on the counter and gave it a friendly pat. "No problem. I'd even be willing to sign that as part of our agreement."

Mattie stared at him. She wasn't sure whether she'd made her point or not.

Grant picked up the sheet of paper. "Number four—you want us to find out who was responsible for Mattie Whittaker's death." For the first time, he frowned. "Why do you want to mess around in something that happened fifty years ago?"

He slid from the stool and walked to the window where he could see the highway. How often had he done just this thing as a kid, dreaming about getting away? "Look, I know that you think of Mattie Whittaker as some kind of friendly spirit, or whatever—" he waved a hand "—some ghost who plays the harpsichord, opens doors, moves urns around." He turned back to her. "But I've been used to thinking of her—when I did, in my less rational moments—as the woman who

put a curse on this whole town and drove everyone away."
He raised a hand to stop Mattie's interruption. "I know, I
know. We've been using her as a scapegoat for our problems. But to tell you the truth, I'm tired of believing in any of
it. Maybe it all ought to stop right here and now. Nothing we
do will change what happened to Mattie Whittaker. What I
want to do is concentrate on the present, getting custody of
J.D. and turning your restaurant into the best country inn in
upstate New York."

How could she argue? Mattie studied him for a moment,
thinking of her father's murder and how it had affected, and
still affected, each member of her family. "You're right," she
finally said. "It's the present that has to be our priority, but
sometimes the past has a way of reaching out and interfer-
ing."

"What do you mean?" Grant asked.

With two fingers she pulled the anonymous note out of her
pouch. She'd sealed it into a plastic bag, and she turned to
smooth it out on the counter. In two strides, Grant was behind her, reading over her shoulder.

"*Leave Barclayville?* When did you get this?"

"Last night, after you called. And there was a phone call
on Friday night."

"What does Delaney think?"

"I haven't told him."

Grant grabbed her shoulders and turned her on the stool
so she was facing him. "Someone called you, left you a note,
and you haven't told the sheriff?"

"I was going to . . ." Her voice trailed away when she saw
the look in his eyes. She'd seen his anger once before, the night
she'd refused his partnership offer, but what she felt radiating from him now was even more potent.

"Look, I own the property. And as long as I do, I am responsible for your safety. So we're going to take reasonable

precautions. And that means keeping the sheriff informed. Clear?" He pulled her off the stool. "Let's go."

Mattie snatched the note and zipped it into her pouch as he dragged her with him out of the diner. When they reached his motorcycle, she dug in her heels.

"It's ten miles to Delaney's office in Mason's Corners—a long walk." He put on his helmet, then unhooked the spare and settled it on her head. "Your choice," he said and mounted the bike. He started the engine.

Mattie barely had time to climb up behind him before they were spraying gravel on the way out of the parking lot.

Grant opened up the throttle. He needed a fast ride to rid himself of the emotions rolling through him, to regain some control. It was more than the fact that she hadn't yet told Delaney about the threats. What had his blood boiling was the thought of her alone in that house, with only some eccentric, female version of Casper to protect her while someone scared her with crank calls and threatening notes. What he wouldn't give to get his hands on the person.... He whipped the bike around a truck filled with hay and accelerated.

Any thought Mattie had of sitting primly behind Grant with her hands holding his hips for balance had vanished about thirty seconds away from the parking lot, when she'd wrapped her arms around him and held on for dear life. Her heart had lodged itself in her throat for a while, but as soon as she could open her eyes, she realized she was enjoying the ride.

It was fun. The speed, the freedom, the wind whipping against her skin, the vibration of the bike beneath her and the risk that added the spice of fear to the adventure. She liked all of it, but it was the excitement of everything combined that was seducing her. It was like a good recipe, with each ingredient being an essential element of the total effect.

She started to relax, to let her mind drift, leaning automatically with Grant into the curves. And though she'd left it out of the recipe she'd been thinking of, she had to admit that she also liked the feel of her body pressed against his. Visual impressions she'd gathered of wide shoulders and narrow hips were being reinforced now by touch. There was strength here that she could feel. Warmth, too. She could feel his muscles bunch and relax beneath the thin shirt he was wearing. She couldn't resist resting her head against his back for just a moment.

But it was a mistake. Hadn't she spent days trying to convince herself that she could restrict her dealings with him to business? And here he was already demonstrating how much pleasure could intrude into their little arrangement.

The wildflowers growing along the road blurred into a continuous ribbon of royal blue, and Mattie felt the sudden burst of power and speed beneath her as Grant whipped past another truck. She tightened her hold on him and laughed.

GRANT WAS CALMER by the time they reached the outskirts of Mason's Corners. He might have felt even more calm if he could have convinced himself that it was the speed of the ride alone that had drained away some of his rage. The truth was, though, his anger hadn't so much disappeared as it had been shoved aside by other feelings. Conflicting feelings. Feelings that had been running through him from the moment Mattie wrapped her arms around him.

Desire was the easiest to identify. He wanted Mattie. Of that he was very sure. He also wanted to protect her. That emotion, too, he could recognize because he felt the same way about J.D. And yet it wasn't exactly the same. With Mattie it was both simpler and more complicated. With her, he didn't just want, he *needed*.

He was still reeling from the thought as he drove into the parking space next to Mac Delaney's truck and smacked into the curb.

Mattie complained, but Grant was already dismounting. He hurried ahead of her into the sheriff's office.

Mac had his chair leaning back, his long legs crossed at the ankles and propped on a desk that was old enough to qualify as an antique and beat-up enough to be correctly categorized as junk. He dog-eared the corner of a page and put down the paperback he'd been reading.

"Busy day?" Grant asked.

"Actually, it's been quite hectic. I had to collar a couple of nine-year-olds who decided to celebrate the end of term by throwing bricks through the school windows."

Grant glanced at the two empty cells.

"Plea bargain," Mac explained. "I don't tell their parents and they come here every Saturday and clean the place."

Grant let his gaze sweep the room as he crossed to the desk "I think I would have preferred jail." He glanced down at the title of the book Mac had just put down. "Horror?"

"I have to relieve my boredom somehow."

Grant saw his friend's gaze shift past his shoulder, then brighten. "Ms. Farrell." Mac unfolded himself from his chair. "It's a pleasure. I didn't see you come in."

Grant stepped into Mac's line of vision. "Stick to your book, my friend."

Mac shot Grant a speculative look and then gave him a brief nod before he pulled a file out of his top drawer. "I've got the reports ready for your signatures."

"Reports?" Grant asked.

"You were supposed to drop by today and sign them," Mac said, handing him a pen.

"Oh, yeah." Grant scribbled his name, then passed the pen to Mattie.

"But I can see that's not what you're here for. Have a seat."

Mattie perched on the edge of a padded chair that had lost half its stuffing.

Grant began to pace. "Someone's threatening Mattie. They called on Friday night and dropped off a note on Sunday."

Mattie placed the sealed plastic bag on Mac's desk.

"Imagine that. It's been years since anyone's had to be encouraged to leave Barclayville." He examined the note, then leaned back in his chair and pursed his lips thoughtfully.

"I don't like it," Grant said.

"I don't much care for it myself." Mac looked at Mattie. "Did you recognize the voice?"

She shook her head. "It was distorted, and my Call I.D. box didn't pick up a number because it wasn't a local call."

Mac leaned forward to take another look at the note. "I'll send it to the state lab and have it checked for prints, but unless our anonymous author has a record, we won't get an identification that way, either. However, it does tell us that someone is unhappy about the discovery of those two skeletons."

"Two?" Mattie and Grant spoke the word together.

Mac drew another paper out of the file. "Seems one was bricked up behind the other, and one set of bones showed more deterioration, leading the coroner to conclude that the bodies were buried at different times, a few years apart at least. Both were females in their late teens or early twenties and both had broken necks."

"The murderer used the fireplace twice?" Mattie asked.

Mac shrugged. "It worked the first time."

Grant pulled a chair around and straddled it. "And they both had their necks broken."

"The cellar stairs come to mind," Mac said.

"Oh, my God." Mattie glanced at Grant. "The urn. You don't suppose . . ."

Mac looked from one to the other of them. "Would one of you like to explain?"

"It's a long story," Grant said. "There've been some strange things going on at Whittaker House that Mattie believes my great-aunt may be responsible for."

"Your great-aunt the ghost?" Mac asked.

"She's always moving an urn of flowers to block the stairs," Mattie said. "Maybe to warn me."

"I'll keep it in mind," Mac said. "But it's not really the kind of evidence I can take to court. And they didn't have to fall down stairs. There are other ways to break a neck."

"We could be talking about a serial killer," Grant said.

Mac glanced up at him. "I wouldn't go that far."

"Did you identify the victims?" Mattie asked.

"We're checking dental records. It'll take time and luck." Mac opened an envelope and placed a locket and a ring on his desk blotter. "You recognize either of these?"

Mattie picked up the locket and turned it over in the palm of her hand. Two interlocking hearts. Unusual. And even in its tarnished condition, she could see the intricate design carved into the gold, the repeated pattern of interconnected hearts. Inside was a tiny picture, the images too faded with time to be recognizable. She handed it to Grant and picked up the ring, a sapphire surrounded with diamonds. She felt the warmth immediately and smelled lilacs. "It's hers."

"Whose?" Mac asked.

"She thinks it belongs to my great-aunt Mattie because she smells lilacs." Grant didn't want to admit that he could smell them too.

"I'm afraid I need more than that," Mac said, slipping the jewelry back into an envelope.

"How are you going to get what you need?" Mattie asked.

"I'll visit some of our senior citizens and maybe I'll get lucky. That sapphire looks like an engagement ring. If it belonged to Mattie Whittaker, I'm willing to bet she would have shown it off."

"And what do you plan to do about the person who's threatening Mattie?" Grant asked.

"Not much I *can* do but wait."

"For what? For something worse to happen?"

"I can drive by the place, check on it regularly." Mac turned to Mattie. "Other than that, I can only caution you to be careful. And you might want to consider postponing your plans to work on the Barclay mansion."

"No." Grant and Mattie spoke together.

"Then be careful." He waited until they were at the door. "And leave the detective work to me."

GRANT PULLED IN to the driveway of Whittaker House and parked the bike behind Mattie's red Toyota. This time, the ride had cleared his head. He'd made his decision. Mac may have decided on a wait-and-see approach, but Grant couldn't. There was too much at stake.

Mattie scrambled off the bike, handed him the helmet and went to inspect her car. "It's got four new tires!" she exclaimed.

"Reasonable precautions. I want my partner to be safe. You would agree that the success of the inn depends on your being around to run it?"

"Yes, but that doesn't mean that you should be buying—"

He interrupted her. "I consider it a necessary business expense. And speaking of business, we need to settle some things between us." He glanced at the house.

"You smelled the lilacs, didn't you?" she demanded as she walked with him across the lawn.

The door swung open on cue. The harpsichord began to play. Grant ignored the urn on his way into the front parlor.

When he turned, Mattie was so close that she took a quick step back.

"You're not going to keep out of it, are you?" he asked.

"No. You smelled those lilacs. Don't bother to deny it. And I think Mac is right about the ring. Someone will know—" Her face lit up. "Of course! Ada Mae and Lily!"

Grant grabbed her wrist and settled her on the sofa. "Before you go rushing off to investigate a fifty-year-old murder, we're going to finish our partnership negotiations."

"I thought we already did."

"You've inserted your stipulations. I have a few of my own," he said, shoving his hands into the back pockets of his jeans. "And you're right. I did smell lilacs." He shot a quick look at the portrait as "Mendelssohn's Wedding March" swelled to a crescendo in the dining room. "I'm not sure that I believe in her the way you do, but something's going on here. Anyway, it isn't a ghost calling you up or sending you notes. And I don't want anything to happen to you." He brought his hands out of his pockets and folded his arms across his chest. "These are my terms. Number one, if you insist on poking your nose into two murders, we're going to do it together as partners. Deal?"

Mattie nodded. "Deal."

It was only as she agreed that he realized how tense he was. He rubbed at the knot in the back of his neck. "Number two, we're going to take reasonable precautions about your safety. Until Mac straightens this out, you're not staying alone in this house." He pointed to the sofas. "I'll sleep on one of these—"

"I don't think that's such a good idea."

"I've agreed to all of your conditions, even the one about our relationship being strictly business. And I'll keep my word on that until you change your mind. But until we find out what happened to my great-aunt, I'm your houseguest. Take it or leave it, partner." He extended his hand.

After a moment's hesitation, Mattie put her hand in his.

He smiled and he pulled her to her feet. "I know just how we can christen our new partnership."

"In your dreams, Whittaker." Taking her hand back, she moved past him. "I'm going to call Ada Mae."

"I've got a better idea. Strictly business, I promise."

Standing in the archway, she turned back.

"There's this friend of mine, Carlotta Strong, who runs the Shallow Creek Inn in Haverford. She'll be our closest competition, so from a strictly business angle, we ought to check her out. Not only does she serve the best soul food north of the Mason-Dixon line, but she comes from a long line of great chefs. Her grandmother used to be the cook at the Barclay mansion every summer when the Barclays were in residence. She just might recognize the locket."

Mattie glanced down at her clothes. "I'll have to change."

Grant felt the last of his tension seep away as he followed her into the foyer and watched her race up the stairs.

A HALF AN HOUR LATER, Mattie parked the Toyota in front of the Shallow Creek Inn. She'd insisted on taking her car and won, much to her surprise. Carlotta Strong's restaurant surprised her, too. A picture-perfect little farmhouse, painted bright blue with white shutters and an L-shaped porch lined with pots of red geraniums, it was smaller than Whittaker House and set farther back from the road.

Mattie caught the tantalizing aroma of fresh-baked bread and heard a loud, lusty laugh, when Grant led her through the door, into the lobby. She had only a moment to absorb a barrage of colors and textures—lacy, white tie-back curtains framing the windows, splashy red and blue tulips in the cushions covering the window seat, the stenciled wallpaper.

The room was small and almost completely filled by the old-
fashioned hotel-registration desk. She would have been
tempted to run her hand over the gleaming dark mahogany
if it hadn't been for the large tiger-striped cat stretched out
there, eyeing them curiously.

"Grant Whittaker!"

Mattie turned to see a large, dark-skinned woman bearing
down on them. She was wearing an ankle-length, blue ging-
ham dress with a white ruffled apron and a matching cap that
was barely managing to keep her mop of curls in check.

"A bad penny always turns up!" She enveloped Grant in a
warm hug and then stepped back to study him. "I heard you
were back in town, and I was beginning to think that I would
have to send out an engraved invitation."

"Carlotta, I'd like you to meet Mattie Farrell."

Mattie found herself looking into large, chocolate brown
eyes lit with warmth and humor. The tiny lines fanning out
from the corners of those eyes and the sprinkle of gray in the
curls were the only clues Mattie could find to the woman's
age. And even then she couldn't have guessed.

"Of Whittaker House." Carlotta took Mattie's hands in
hers. "I've heard nothing but good things about you, child."
She winked. "Your taste's improving, Grant. About time."
She led them through the first dining room to a sun room with
two walls of windows looking out on the garden. "This will
be more private." Laying her hand on Grant's shoulder, she
turned to Mattie. "Running a restaurant was a midlife career
change for me, so I needed a lot of advice. Grant was my
consultant. The decor, the landscaping, even the first
course . . . he helped with all of it. He also suggested we start
off each of our dinners with hush puppies and corn bread.
The entrée tonight is fried chicken with mashed potatoes and
collard greens. And we have lemon meringue pie for dessert.
Save room for it. It's my grandmother's recipe. The lemon-

ade's on the house. But my son Ben just sent me five cases of a nice California chardonnay that I can highly recommend."

"We'll take a bottle," Grant said, "and we'll save a glass for you when you can join us."

"You've got a date, handsome." Chuckling, Carlotta hurried off to answer the jangle of an insistent bell.

"This is lovely," Mattie said. She drew in a deep breath and caught the scent of fresh flowers mixed with hot candle wax and above it the aroma of food. Familiar smells. She felt comfortable and easy in Grant's company and leaned toward him. "And you very nearly had me convinced that you didn't believe in creating atmosphere. I was beginning to believe that you were hung up on blue-plate specials."

He smiled and reached over to take her hand. "As far as atmosphere goes, I've always appreciated variety. In a diner, the pleasures are always quick and hot. In a place like this, they can linger on and on . . . Which do you prefer?"

Mattie found that her mouth had suddenly gone dry. The atmosphere that she'd found so relaxing a few seconds ago had faded until all she was aware of was Grant—his smile, his touch. She wasn't even aware that the waiter had poured the wine until Grant released her hand to raise his glass in a toast.

"To our partnership."

"To the successful expansion of Whittaker House." Mattie sipped her wine, and delighted with the taste, sipped again. "I wonder if Carlotta's son could get some of this for us."

"Is your mind always on business?" he asked.

Her smile was a little rueful. "Maybe it's because I was raised in a restaurant."

"That might be reason enough for some people to run away."

"Not me. I loved it. But I learned early on that I didn't want to be just a chef. I wanted to run the show. And I wanted to do it on my own. That's one of the reasons I left Syracuse. If I'd stayed, I'd probably still be working for my mother or at least in her shadow." She met his eyes over the rim of her wineglass. "What about you? Was the diner one of the reasons you had to get away from Barclayville?"

"No. I actually loved the diner. Living with George, working with him . . . those were happy times for me. Anything I know about being a father, I learned from him. When he discovered that I had a real love for school, he encouraged me to study and go on to college. And I always knew I was going to leave here. Having the same name as a curse was a good incentive, and maybe I had to prove that I could do something on my own, too."

Just then, the waiter set a huge plate of hush puppies in front of her. "Good heavens!" Mattie explained.

Grant took one, broke it in half and poured syrup over it.

"That looks sinful," she said.

He held out a forkful, then enjoyed watching her eyes close as she bit into it and savored the taste. "I'll share," he offered when she was looking at him again.

"Not on your life." She reached for one of her own.

Grant liked watching her eat. She would break off one piece at a time, then neatly dribble the syrup on it with such focus, as if each separate bite was a unique experience to be savored, then stored away for future reference. Is that the way she would make love, too? he wondered. How would it feel to be at the center of that precision, that total concentration? And what would it be like to break it?

"Are you thinking what I'm thinking?" Mattie asked.

"Hmm?"

"That we ought to ask Carlotta for the recipe."

Grant laughed. "Even if you were able to charm her into it, woman to woman, you wouldn't be able to duplicate it.

She claims that nothing she cooks ever comes out the same way twice."

"Spreading stories about me again?" Carlotta was chuckling as she whisked away the hush puppies. "Keep it up. I want to be a legend in my own time." When she set down a platter piled high with fried chicken, she turned to Mattie. "Don't worry, child. You won't offend me if you don't clean the plate. I remember when I was your age, before I married Martin Strong, I had a tiny waist like yours. Anything you don't finish, I can pack up for you to take along with you."

Before Carlotta had sailed out of the room, Mattie was digging into her first piece. Two pieces later, she wiped her lips with her napkin and leaned slowly back in her chair. "I can't eat another bite. I'm not sure I can even walk out of here."

"Dessert?" Carlotta poked her head around the archway.

Mattie managed a moan. Grant shook his head.

"I'll just have them pack it up with the rest of the chicken. It'll make a nice picnic lunch." Drawing up a chair, Carlotta lowered herself into it with a sigh. "It's been a long day." She sipped the wine that Grant handed to her. "So when do you plan to open up your inn, Ms. Farrell?"

Mattie and Grant both turned to stare at her. "How did you—"

"Elementary, my dear Whittaker," Carlotta said. "Look at the facts. I got a call from Martha Bickle on Friday afternoon that the Farrell woman and Grant Whittaker were poking around the Barclay mansion and discovered a bunch of bones buried in an old fireplace. I ask myself why the two of you might be spending a lovely afternoon nosing around an old house that everyone's been scared to death of for fifty years, and the answer came to me in a flash." She snapped her fingers. "You're running a successful restaurant, Grant here's a hotel and restaurant consultant. When I add that up, even without my calculator, I get a picture of the Barclay mansion as a country inn. It's the only way to increase business out here in God's country." She patted Mattie's hand. "It'll be perfect, by the way. And I'm jealous that you not only have a ghost, but you've got a skeleton, too. I don't know what I'll do to compete."

Grant looked at Mattie. "Did I mention that before Carlotta decided to go into the restaurant business, she used to put out the weekly paper in Haverford?"

"That's a polite way of saying that I'm the official town gossip." Carlotta explained.

"You've got most of it right," Grant said. "Only I'm not just consulting this time. Mattie and I are partners."

"Congratulations!" Carlotta lifted her glass in a toast. "I should have offered you champagne."

"And Mac Delaney informed us this afternoon that we dug up two skeletons, not one," Mattie added. "And they were buried at different times. One was bricked up behind the other."

"Two?" Carlotta's expression suddenly sobered. "Any idea who they are?"

"Both women in their late teens or early twenties. Mattie and I are pretty sure that one of them is my great-aunt Mattie Whittaker. They found a sapphire ring that might be her engagement ring. But there was a locket, too." Carlotta got a pencil and paper from the sideboard, and handed them to Mattie.

"Make a sketch, and I'll show it to Gran. She's still sharp as a tack. If she saw either piece, she'll remember who wore them." While Mattie drew the pieces of jewelry, Carlotta shook her head. "Two murders gone fifty years without justice. No wonder there's been such trouble."

1

3 WAYS TO PLAY
see inside

for big CASH prizes and FREE GIFTS!

First play your "Win-A-Fortune" game tickets
to qualify for up to

ONE MILLION DOLLARS IN LIFETIME INCOME

– that's $33,333.33 each year for 30 years!

WIN A CASH FORTUNE

Game Ticket values vary. Scratch GOLD from Big Money
Wheel to determine the potential cash value of prize you will
receive if the sweepstakes number assigned to this ticket is a
prize winning number.

GAME TIX NO. **1a**

DO NOT SEPARATE—KEEP ALL GAMES INTACT

WIN A CASH FORTUNE

Game Ticket values vary. Scratch GOLD from Big Money
Wheel to determine the potential cash value of prize you will
receive if the sweepstakes number assigned to this ticket is a
prize winning number.

GAME TIX NO. **1b**

DO NOT SEPARATE—KEEP ALL GAMES INTACT

WIN A CASH FORTUNE

Game Ticket values vary. Scratch GOLD from Big Money
Wheel to determine the potential cash value of prize you will
receive if the sweepstakes number assigned to this ticket is a
prize winning number.

GAME TIX NO. **1c**

DO NOT SEPARATE—KEEP ALL GAMES INTACT

WIN A CASH FORTUNE

Game Ticket values vary. Scratch GOLD from Big Money
Wheel to determine the potential cash value of prize you will
receive if the sweepstakes number assigned to this ticket is a
prize winning number.

GAME TIX NO. **1d**

DO NOT SEPARATE—KEEP ALL GAMES INTACT

WIN A CASH FORTUNE

Game Ticket values vary. Scratch GOLD from Big Money
Wheel to determine the potential cash value of prize you will
receive if the sweepstakes number assigned to this ticket is a
prize winning number.

GAME TIX NO. **1e**

DO NOT SEPARATE—KEEP ALL GAMES INTACT

FOLD ALONG DOTTED LINE AND DETACH CAREFULLY

With a coin, carefully scratch off the three gold boxes. Then check the chart below to learn how many FREE BOOKS will be yours!

			WORTH FOUR FREE BOOKS!
			WORTH THREE FREE BOOKS!
			WORTH TWO FREE BOOKS!
			WORTH ONE FREE BOOK!

You'll receive four brand-new Harlequin Temptation® novels. When you scratch off the gold boxes and return this card in the reply envelope provided, we'll send you the books you qualify for <u>absolutely free</u>.

JITTERS. Mattie felt them skimming along her nerve endings and tingling in her fingertips as she carried bedding into the front parlor of Whittaker House. She'd have liked to blame the sudden attack of nervousness on Carlotta's words. After all, a two-time murderer had gone free all these years—there was certainly justification for a dandy case of nerves there. She dropped the pile of blankets and sheets on the table. Grant had gone to fetch Hannibal, so she was temporarily alone in the house, but that wasn't what was making her so edgy, either.

Shaking out a sheet, she tossed it over the cushions of the sofa and began to tuck in the corners. No, what had her stomach jumping was that Grant Whittaker was going to be staying in Whittaker House tonight. And making up his bed wasn't calming her down one bit. Just the opposite, in fact. With very little effort, she could picture him lying right in front of her on the sofa, his chest bare, the sheet angled carelessly across one of those long legs of his. She'd seen him sleeping before, that very first day in the hammock. And she recalled how much she'd wanted to touch that smooth skin stretched taut over bone and muscle. How much she'd wanted to feel those muscles move beneath her hands.

She realized that she was massaging one of the pillows and tossed it down on the couch. She couldn't remember ever acting this way about a man before. With Mark Brenner, the relationship had been tidy, organized, something they fit into their busy work schedule. It had run so smoothly that she had never once suspected that romancing her was just part of Mark's plan to take over the inn. She frowned thoughtfully. With Grant, she felt as if she were on a roller-coaster ride, never knowing what to expect at the top of the next precipice. Except a fall.

Slowly, she sank onto the sofa and linked her fingers together in her lap. Could this be what falling in love felt like?

GRANT HAD BEEN WATCHING her from the foyer for some time. The front door had opened for him, and the harpsichord was playing something soft and romantic. The lights were soft, too, shining on her hair and skin. She looked so right sitting there beneath the portrait of his great-aunt. As if she belonged. Something moved through him then. Not desire, not anything as simple as that. For just a moment, he almost felt as if he had come home.

Mattie rose and turned to spread a blanket on the cushions. As Grant watched, the scene in front of him blurred, and a new one formed. The sheets and blankets were suddenly rumpled, cushions scattered across the floor, and he and Mattie lay tangled together on the sofa. Wind rattled the windows and flames crackled in the fireplace. She was above him, her hair falling free and brushing against his skin, burning brighter than the fire.

She glanced up then and saw him. "I didn't hear you." She raised a hand, then dropped it. "This sofa's a love seat. It won't be very comfortable."

"I've slept in worse places," he said, glancing down at the bed she'd made, but it wasn't sleep or comfort he was thinking of. When he moved toward her, he saw desire in her eyes, and nervousness.

He moved closer and she stepped away, but her retreat ended when she felt the mantel at her back. She could have stopped him when she felt his hands grip her waist. She could have pushed past him and walked out of the room. But she didn't.

He had such strong hands. She felt the pressure of each one of those long, slender fingers as they slid slowly up her ribs to rest along the sides of her breasts.

He didn't kiss her. The promise was in his eyes, but he didn't kiss her. She could still remember what it had been like the last time—the heat, the whirlwind of sensations. The memory alone had her breath quickening and her lips parting.

But this time when he fit his mouth to hers, it was very different. There was no demanding this time, only invitation, impossible to resist as his tongue moved over her lips. His taste was different, too. Darker, richer than she recalled. And then suddenly, the thinking part of her brain shut off. All she knew was she wanted more. She rose on tiptoe, lifted her hands to frame his face and pulled him closer.

So different, Grant thought as he shifted the angle of the kiss and began to deepen it slowly. There had been a honey-eyed sweetness in her taste that he'd dreamed about and begun to crave, but her flavor was wilder, more tempting than he remembered. Perhaps there would always be something new to savor in her response. Maybe even after years and years, he'd still react to the way her breath hitched when he nipped at her bottom lip, the way she shuddered when he moved his hand to cup her breast. Even as he took his fill, he wondered if he would ever have enough of her taste. Or the softness of her skin, which tempted him even through the thin material of her blouse.

He was fumbling with her buttons when she breathed his name. The sound, the helplessness of it, had him drawing back. In the back of his mind, he remembered quite clearly the agreement they'd made. When they did make love, he wanted her to be as willing as he was.

When her eyes were clear and focused on his, he said, "We're going to make love on this love seat."

Mattie pushed away the image. "I can't see where we're going, you and I."

"I already told you. We're going to make love right here in this room. Many times." Even as he said it, he knew it was true.

"I mean where we're going to end. When I start down a path, I like to know where it's going to end."

She hadn't contradicted him, nor had she argued, Grant noticed. They were making progress. He grinned at her. "What's the fun in knowing the ending?"

"The *fun* is you can plan ahead and be prepared."

"Life isn't like that, Mattie. It's packed full of surprises. Haven't you ever heard of no risk, no reward?" He dropped a friendly kiss on her nose before he sank onto the love seat and stretched out.

Mattie didn't dare look down at him. She kept her gaze straight ahead, hoping that her legs would work well enough to get her up the stairs. She saved her sigh of relief until she closed the door of her room.

6

SHE'D OVERSLEPT. Something she rarely did. But then, she'd been awake most of the night thinking about Grant Whittaker and what she was going to do about him.

She gave herself a shake as she hurried down the stairs. The problem wasn't what to do about Grant. It was what to do about herself. If he'd broken their agreement, so had she. When he'd kissed her last night, she'd kissed him right back.

She could have stopped it, pulled back, run! Why hadn't she? Because for just a moment, she'd felt something more than passion, or desire, or need. Something just out of reach . . .

At the foot of the stairs, she turned and walked into the front parlor. It was empty. Not that she'd expected him to be there. It was almost eight, and he had to open the diner before seven. The only sign that he'd spent the night was the neat pile of bedding on the table. And a note. She hurried to pick it up.

Mattie, did you dream of me? Since I know you'll wake up with business on your mind, here's a list of local contractors you can call for estimates.

Grant

There were eight names and phone numbers. Mattie's eyes narrowed as she looked at the list. While she'd woken up wondering, worrying about a kiss, Grant had obviously been able to keep *his* mind on business!

She jammed the paper into her pocket and headed for the kitchen. As she passed the harpsichord, it erupted into a trill.

Mattie glared at it. "Don't even start. Not until I've had my coffee." In the kitchen doorway, she turned back. "He left me a list of things to do. Can you imagine? Maybe in the academic world, the word *partner* means a secretary, or wife, but—"

The instant she said the word *wife*, the harpsichord segued from a trill into the wedding march.

Whirling, Mattie shut the door firmly behind her. *Coffee.* It was the only way to clear her head so that she could think rationally about her problem. She stuffed a filter into the pot and measured grounds. Talking to a ghost wasn't going to help.

Once she was inhaling caffeine fumes, Mattie began to feel a little better. All she needed to do was find a way to handle Grant Whittaker.

With a moan, she leaned her elbows on the sink and dropped her forehead onto her fists. Wrong word, *wrong word!* The exact problem she had to solve was wanting to *handle* Grant Whittaker every time he came anywhere near her!

The coffeepot made a last, sputtering gasp, and Mattie reached for a mug. "You've got to get a grip," she muttered.

In the dining room, the harpsichord played several woeful chords in a minor key. Ignoring it, Mattie turned to stare out the window. There had to be a way out of the mess she'd gotten herself into. If she could just sort through it. Logically. Logic had always been her ally in the past.

She drained her mug and refilled it. The expansion of the inn had to be her first priority. Reaching into her pocket, she pulled out a piece of paper, grabbed a pencil from the stash that Ada Mae kept in her drawer and wrote down the Whittaker Inn as number one. Number two, she and Grant had to solve a fifty-year-old mystery. No small task, she mused as she tapped the pencil on the sink. And number three, she had to keep her feelings for Grant Whittaker under control. It occurred to her that though she'd succeeded in prioritizing things, she'd also listed them in order of increasing difficulty.

Number one. She drew a circle around it. When the phone rang, she lifted the receiver. "Whittaker House."

"Mattie."

Her lips had curved in a smile before she could tell herself she wasn't happy to hear his voice.

"Did you read the note I left?"

"Yes." She heard the clatter of plates and silverware in the background.

"Well, did you dream of me?"

"No." It was the truth, and it gave her great pleasure to say it with conviction.

"So I kept you awake, huh?"

"In your dreams, Whittaker."

"You've got that right."

She'd never realized before that it was possible to hear a grin over a telephone wire. Could he hear hers, too? She looked down at the paper she still held and tried to remember the priorities she'd listed there. "About your list . . ."

"I knew you'd like it. Because of the way you always put business before pleasure. That's how I knew you'd want to get started as soon as possible. But you've probably got people in Syracuse that you're thinking of using. If they come in with a competitive estimate on the work, then we'll give it to them, of course. But it wouldn't hurt to hire local people if we can."

"I agree," Mattie said. It made sense. It also meant that she and Grant were thinking along the same lines in terms of priorities.

"You don't mind making the calls?"

"No. I was just getting ready to dial the first number."

"Great. That will give us time to go visit the Clemson sisters this afternoon. You know, I think this partnership thing is going to work in my favor."

"How's that?" Mattie asked.

"If we're working together like this all day, sooner or later, I'm going to slip into your dreams at night."

She hung up the phone, but not before she heard his grin turn into a laugh.

THREE HOURS LATER, Mattie had made the acquaintance of several of the area's more talkative residents. Some were more enthusiastic about the renovation plans than others, but all were willing to share their views. One carpenter was so excited about the idea of working on the old house that he'd said he would stop over late that afternoon.

She'd scheduled all the others for appointments the following week, except for one painter who'd flat out refused to have anything to do with the Barclay mansion and had proceeded to explain why for forty-five minutes.

Mattie set Grant's list on the counter, then flipped it over and looked at her own. If only it would be as easy to get through. She put a little check by number one. At least, she and Grant had made a start. Then she looked at number two and remembered Grant's invitation to visit the Clemsons. Paying calls on Mattie Whittaker's contemporaries was one way to investigate the case. But, she thought as she tapped her pencil thoughtfully on the paper, the Barclay mansion itself might provide some clue. As early as this afternoon, the first workman would be walking through the place. In a week or so, it would be filled with work crews, and something might be destroyed.

Mattie looked at her watch. She had over an hour before Grant would be back from the diner. Grabbing her pouch off a hook, she fastened it around her waist, hurried out the door and walked to the Barclay mansion.

She was struck by how peaceful the old house looked, as if it were totally oblivious to the tragedy that had occurred within its walls.

Sun glinted off the windows, and Mattie thought she saw something moving in one of the dormers on the third floor. It had to be in the servants' wing. Maybe it was just a trick of the light. An old curtain ruffled by a stray breeze pushing its way through a broken pane of glass? Shading her eyes with her hand, she moved forward. Whatever it was, she didn't see it again.

She entered the mansion through the French doors that opened into the main parlor. She hadn't taken three steps when she heard a board creak loudly overhead. She stopped and listened for a count of ten, then hurried into the wide foyer. Somewhere upstairs she heard the soft metallic click of a door shutting.

"Hello?" she called up the stairs. When there was no response, she tried again, "Hello." It was too early for the carpenter she'd spoken to. She hadn't seen a car, either. With a frown, she started to climb to the second floor. Keeping to the edge of each step, she listened for something, anything.

When she reached the top, Mattie turned to look down the curved stairway. Silly to be so nervous. Old houses made noises. A draft could easily blow a door shut. Even as the thought occurred, she suddenly felt cold. Curious, she walked down three steps and then back up. It was slightly cooler near the carved post at the top of the stairs. She'd never noticed that before.

Sitting down, she wrapped her arms around her knees. The house was quiet now. Not even the dust motes were moving. They seemed to hang suspended in the light that had battled its way into the foyer. Then she heard another board creak.

She straightened her shoulders in an attempt to ignore the little sliver of fear crawling up her spine. She'd come here to find a hint—something, anything that would give her a clue about what really happened in this house fifty years ago. To do that she had to open herself to it, let her mind drift the way she did when she was trying to identify some ingredient in a recipe. It wouldn't work if she was acting like a nervous ninny, jumping at every noise, letting her imagination run amok.

She gripped the carved post to pull herself up and as she did, she felt the scratches that marred the bottom of the banister. She made a mental note to tell the carpenter about them as she started down the stairs. If she was looking for hints or premonitions or some other form of ghostly communication about what had happened to Mattie Whittaker all those years ago, the cellar was probably the place to go.

Before she could talk herself out of it, Mattie opened the door as wide as she could and took the flashlight out of her pouch. She aimed the light low as she crept down the cellar stairs, hugging the wall for support. Every step groaned or creaked. At the bottom, she began to shiver.

It was very cold. And not because of any ghost, she told herself as she felt her way along the stone wall. Cellars in old houses were always cold. They were used to store food. And wine. She could use a glass of wine right now. Just as soon as she was back at Whittaker House, Mattie promised herself that she would have one, maybe two.

The first thing she picked up in the beam from her flashlight was the cavernous opening of the fireplace. Though she could have walked right into it, she didn't, but she did step closer to take a better look. The pile of bricks next to it was all that remained to show that the fireplace had once been a tomb. Otherwise, it looked exactly like what it was, a large fireplace where meals had once been prepared. Then Mattie caught the scent of lilacs.

A door slammed like the crack of a rifle shot, and she dropped the flashlight. The glass smashed and then there was only the sound of the metal rolling away from her in the darkness. She couldn't scream, not while her heart was lodged in her throat. Whirling, she groped her way to the foot of the stairs. She waited, listening. At first, she heard only her own ragged breathing. Then footsteps moving slowly and steadily overhead. Quite clearly, she could picture the path they were taking across the foyer.

"Hey!" she called out. "You've shut me in!"

The footsteps continued. Then she heard another door close. Maybe they couldn't hear her. They? No, she was not going to think about who had just walked across the foyer. First she was going to get herself out of the cellar.

All she had to do was get up the stairs and she'd be free. Keeping her back flat against the wall, she edged her way up one step at a time. There were so many of them. Why hadn't she noticed that before? She began to count them to keep herself from thinking about how far each one was taking her from the cellar floor. Then she remembered what Mac had said about stairs and the two young women who had died of broken necks. If she tripped and fell . . . ?

The breath she released was a sob when her hand finally closed around the doorknob. It twisted but didn't open. She tried again, but it held fast. Turning, she gripped the knob with both hands and threw her full weight against the door. It still didn't budge.

Mattie felt panic stream through her veins and bubble up in her throat. Giving in to it, she pounded, kicked and yelled until her hands were stinging and her throat was raw. Then she twisted, pushed and shoved, again and again. Only when she was totally exhausted did she sink onto the top step and drop her head into her hands. No one was going to hear her. Not even Grant would think to look for her here.

Her mind drifted to the other two women who had lain trapped and forgotten in the darkness below her for fifty years. No one had ever thought of looking for them.

But they had been dead. She wasn't. At the very worst, she was scared. And that wouldn't be fatal, unless she gave in to the fear. Someone was certainly hoping she would. That thought set off a little flame of anger deep within her.

She sat there staring into the darkness, thinking. *Someone* had locked her in the cellar. She recalled those earlier sounds she'd heard. The floorboard creaking overhead, the sound of a door clicking shut. It hadn't been a ghost. Of that she was sure. And whoever it was had been clever, hiding in the house, biding their time to scare her.

The fact that they'd succeeded made her even more angry. And part of her anger was directed at herself. Rising, she made her way down the stairs. It might be easier to sit and cower at the top, hoping for rescue, but there were windows in the cellar. She was going to get herself out.

She placed her hand once more on the cold stone wall to guide herself and then nearly screamed when she walked into a faceful of cobwebs. After swatting them away and dragging them off her arm, she moved as quickly as she could toward the first patch of light she could make out.

The window was three feet beyond the reach of her arm and small. Mattie moved to the next one. It wasn't any bigger. Then she caught the scent of lilacs, and knew she wasn't alone.

Think. She searched her mind for something, anything in the cellar that she could use, and remembered the pile of bricks.

One armload at a time, she stacked them against the wall. She felt as if she was in kindergarten. The thought made her smile until a brick toppled off the pile in her arms and landed on her foot. The pain brought instant tears to her eyes. She blinked them away and carried fewer bricks the next time.

By the tenth trip, her muscles were protesting and her back hurt. She stopped counting after that and simply continued to haul and build one layer after another. She wasn't even aware of exactly when the cellar had ceased to feel cold and she had begun to sweat.

When the stack of bricks against the wall was tall enough, she started to build another pile in front of it. This one didn't have to be as high. The third and fourth ones were even shorter. The last one only came up to her knees.

Pausing a minute to catch her breath, Mattie ran her hands over the steps she had created, trying to imprint them on her mind before she placed her foot carefully on the top of the lowest stack and hoisted herself up. With her hands pressed flat against the stone wall and her fingers seeking out and pressing into any available crevice, she found the next foothold. On the third level, she felt the bricks begin to shift and sway. A few crashed to the floor below. Flattening herself against the wall, she closed her eyes and pictured pitching into the darkness with them, breaking something and lying on that cold floor until someone found her.

Ruthlessly, she shoved the image aside and climbed higher. Finally, she grabbed the window latch, and pulled herself up. It came loose in her hand. She teetered, struggling to maintain her balance. Just as she thought she'd lost it, she felt a strong push from behind, and suddenly she was flat against the wall with the window in front of her face.

Not even daring to breathe, she slipped her fingers beneath the window's edge and ducked her head to draw it open. It moved outward like a transom. With both hands, she gripped the ledge.

She smelled earth and fresh air warmed by the sun. And lilacs. She was nearly giddy with the scent. She levered herself up until her shoulders were through the opening, her legs dangling in space. Behind her, she heard an avalanche of bricks crashing to the floor. Using every ounce of strength she had, she brought her knee up and pushed it over the ledge. Then she dug her fingers into the dirt, wiggling and pulling until inch by inch, she dragged herself out.

Exhausted and aching all over, she lay on her back with her eyes closed. After the clammy coldness of the cellar, she relished the heat of the sun beating down on her. Just for a minute, maybe two, she wasn't going to move except to breathe. A breeze carried the scent of dried grass. Nearby, a bumblebee buzzed. She didn't have the energy to open her eyes. If it stung her, she wasn't sure she would have the strength to jump.

Then she heard Grant calling her name.

"Over here," she called, surprised at how weak her voice sounded.

Hannibal reached her first, skidding to a halt a few inches from her head. He sniffed her forehead with his cold nose, then lapped her cheek with his tongue. Before she could brush him away, her shoulders were gripped hard and she was suddenly sitting up staring into Grant's eyes.

"Are you all right?" He gave her a little shake. When he'd first seen her lying on the ground, his heart had stopped beating, and it only started again when her eyes focused clearly on his. "What the hell happened?"

"I'm fine." Mattie reached to brush hair out of her eyes. "I'll be even better when I find out who locked me—"

"You're not fine." Grant took her hand and held it in front of her nose. "You're bleeding."

Mattie stared at the blood, then shook her head impatiently. "It's nothing. I must have scraped myself on the bricks."

"Bricks?" Still frowning, Grant rocked back on his heels. Then her earlier words finally registered. "Who locked you up? Where?"

"In the cellar. And if I knew, I wouldn't be sitting here in the dirt. I'd be making them pay."

Grant's voice rose as he pulled her to her feet. "You went down in the cellar?"

Mattie drew in a deep breath. "If you'd stop shouting questions at me, I could explain." And she told him everything.

Mattie wasn't aware how tightly her fingers were gripping Grant's, but he was. Still, he didn't see any trace of fear in her eyes. "You didn't see anyone?" he asked.

"I heard them. Whoever it was didn't bother to tiptoe once I was down in that cellar. They wanted me to know that I wasn't alone in the house." She tilted her head to one side. "You believe me, don't you?"

He glanced down at her hands. They were small and elegant, the kind of hands a man dreamed of feeling on his body, and they were smeared with dirt and her own blood. The fury that had begun to burn through him while she was talking had settled in his stomach like a hard knot.

"Yeah," he said grimly as he pulled her with him around the corner to the front of the house. "I'm going to check the house." Anything to shove away the image lodged in his mind of someone stalking Mattie through the old mansion. Even worse was imagining the makeshift stairway she'd built. He'd gotten a close look at those bricks the day that Mac Delaney's men had dragged them out of the fireplace. The mortar had decayed long ago into dust, and some of the bricks weren't far behind. Grant deposited Mattie unceremoniously on the porch steps. There would be a time and place to vent his anger. "Stay right here."

She would have protested, but she was too tired to argue anymore. As Hannibal settled himself into a mound at her feet, she patted his head. "I know just how you feel, fella."

Mattie wasn't aware of her eyes drifting shut. She only knew that she had to put some effort into opening them when she heard the crunch of gravel and the low hum of an engine. A sleek, metallic gray sedan pulled to a stop in the driveway.

The man who climbed out wore a suit with a conservative cut that matched the car. Curious, Mattie studied him as he made his way purposefully toward the house. She was willing to bet that he wasn't the carpenter who'd promised to stop by, nor any of the other tradesmen she'd called that morning. As he drew closer, she could see that he was probably in his fifties, and he carried it well. His graying hair was cut short, brushed back off a high forehead. When she rose to stand on the bottom step of the porch, his pale blue eyes behind the wire-rimmed glasses were level with hers; they held a cool but faintly surprised expression.

Mattie smiled. "Can I help you?"

"I'm looking for Ms. Farrell."

"You've found her." Mattie extended her hand.

The man frowned. "You're bleeding."

"It's nothing," Mattie said. "I just scraped my knuckles on some—"

"Stones," Grant interrupted as he stepped through the screen door. "Ms. Farrell was doing a little gardening. Mattie, I'd like you to meet Mr. Desmond from the Merchant's Trust Bank."

"Pete Desmond," the man said, handing Mattie a business card. A brief glance told her that the bank had branches in Utica, Albany and Manhattan.

"Pete stopped by the diner earlier with a very interesting offer. I told him that I never make a move without my partner."

Mattie could hear Grant's anger in the slight emphasis he gave to the word *partner*. She could feel it shimmering out of his body as he moved to stand behind her.

Desmond cleared his throat and directed his gaze to Mattie. "My bank does a lot of work for Amelia Barclay, and she's prepared to make you a very generous cash offer for this property."

Grant placed his hand on Mattie's shoulder. "I told Pete I didn't think we'd be interested in selling."

"No, I'm sorry, but we're not," Mattie said.

Desmond frowned at her. "You haven't even heard the terms."

"You heard my partner's decision," Grant said. "We're not going to sell the Barclay mansion."

Keeping his eyes on Mattie, the banker said, "There are things that you ought to know about this place before you reject Miss Barclay's offer."

"Mattie knows all about the curse," Grant said. "She doesn't believe in it."

"Obviously, I've come at a bad time. You have my card." Desmond gave Mattie a nod before he walked away.

As soon as the car door slammed, Mattie turned to Grant. "Why were you so rude to him?"

"He's a busy man. I just saved him a lot of time. I don't intend to sell this place to Amelia Barclay or anyone else. Not unless we agree to it as *partners*."

"Fine." Hands on hips, she climbed to the top step so she could stand toe-to-toe with him. "I get your not-too-subtle point. You're going out of your way to honor our partnership agreement, and you're implying that I didn't. Why don't you come right out and say it?"

"All right! You broke our agreement when you snuck up here behind my back."

"I didn't sneak!"

Grant looked at her and cursed himself. She was exhausted, bruised and bloody. She looked like something that Hannibal had buried and dug up again, and yet she was ready to do battle. And he was letting her. Cursing himself again, Grant took her arm and pulled her with him.

Mattie dug in her heels. "Where are you—"

"We're going to postpone this discussion until you take a bath and put something on those scrapes."

A HALF AN HOUR LATER, Grant paced in the front parlor of Whittaker House. He could feel his emotions warring inside, much too close to the surface. Anger and frustration, made all the more potent by the fear that was woven through those feelings.

Crossing to the cabinet that served as a bar, he poured brandy into a snifter and took a long swallow. When he'd checked the cellar, he'd found the door bolted. Just as she'd told him, someone had locked her in. That had been enough to bring his blood to a boil. But when he'd gone down the stairs and seen the pile of bricks that lay scattered across the floor... No matter how hard he tried to suppress it, the image of Mattie lying in the midst of that tumble of bricks had continued to lap at the edges of his mind like a persistent wave. He took another sip of brandy and welcomed the way it burned through his system.

He could only imagine what she must have been feeling as she piled them up, the courage it must have had taken to climb them. No, not courage, he thought as he began to pace again. It was just plain, hardheaded foolishness that had inspired her to set foot on that rickety stack of bricks. Or an equally foolish blind faith in some otherworldly spirit.

He glanced up at the picture of his great-aunt. On the surface, the only similarity between the two women was their names. The girl that the painter had captured on canvas was younger than Mattie Farrell. Her hair was more of a honey-gold color with none of the red highlights. Yet there was a set to her shoulders that suggested determination, a look on her face that Joan of Arc might have worn leading her troops into battle. He'd seen the same look in Mattie's eyes. And the girl in the picture was wearing a white dress.

Very slowly, Grant turned around and saw Mattie standing in the archway to the foyer, wearing her usual uniform of white jeans and shirt. The dirt was gone, making her pallor more pronounced. She was wearing bandages on her knuckles and one elbow. He moved to her and drew her over to the sofa. When she was seated, he pressed the brandy glass into her hand. "Drink it. You look like a ghost."

If his words hadn't so aptly described what she was feeling, Mattie might have argued. Instead, she took a sip of brandy, and after a moment a second one.

Grant sat on the sofa across from her. "Why do you always wear white?"

Mattie glanced at him in surprise. "Because it's practical. I'm not a neat cook, but any stain you make will bleach out of white cotton. Why?"

Grant nodded his head toward the portrait. "She's wearing white, too. I don't want you to end up like her. So from now on, you're not to make a move without me."

Mattie set the glass down on the table and stood up. "You're my partner, not my boss. I'm perfectly capable of taking care of myself. After my father died, my brother thought he had the right to tell me what to do. So I moved away from home. And the biggest mistake I made in Maryland was to let my partner have financial control of the inn. That gave him the right to make me sell out to him. I won't take orders from anyone ever again."

Grant rose and crossed to her. "I'm not your last partner. Don't mix me up with him."

"Then don't tell me what to do!"

He grabbed her shoulders and pulled her close. "I'm not going to say a word."

His mouth covered hers and Mattie tasted anger first, then fear. She might have fought against both, but she also tasted his need. And that she couldn't resist, especially when it so clearly reflected her own.

She was lost. Instead of pushing him away, she wound her arms around him and pulled him closer. Straining against him, her body aching with a desire so sweet, she began to anticipate that liberating madness that only he could bring her.

He hadn't intended to touch her. Grant reminded himself of that even as his hands ran over her in one long possessive stroke. It was only as he reassured himself of her softness and strength that his fear finally began to recede. And then all he knew was her taste. So sweet. It reminded him of ice cream, the soft, melting kind that you couldn't eat fast enough on a hot summer day.

He wanted more. Just as he wanted more of the passion he could feel simmering in her just below the surface. And more of the heat that seemed to pump straight from her body into his. He knew even as he took the kiss deeper and felt his needs grow desperate that no matter how much he took, it wouldn't be enough. It was that knowledge that gave him the strength to draw back.

Even as he ended the kiss, Mattie tightened her hold on him. But she felt the change in his touch, the gentling of his hands as he moved them up her arms to frame her face. Then he dropped them to his sides. "I'm sorry."

It wasn't what she wanted to hear. She sank onto the sofa.

Grant ran his hand through his hair as he began to walk back and forth. "Here I am lecturing you on keeping up your end of our agreement, and I . . ."

Mattie stared at him. He was apologizing for something that she'd fully cooperated in. Didn't he know that if he'd pushed her just a little further, kissed her just a little longer, they'd be making love right now? Her gaze shifted to the other sofa. She could almost picture it. Hadn't he told her that they'd make love right in this room? Right there on the sofa?

She reached for the brandy glass and took a long swallow. Did he know how much she wanted to go to him right now and finish what his kiss had started?

Sunlight was pouring into the room, and as he paced, he sent dust motes swirling. That was wrong somehow. And the house was too quiet. Even the harpsichord was silent. The room should be lit with flickering candles, and soft music should be playing. That was the way she'd always imagined it would be when she fell in love.

But then, the feeling was wrong, too. She'd always thought love would be warm and soft. Peaceful. Not scary and edgy and bright like fireworks going off inside with no end in sight.

He had stopped pacing to sit on the sofa across from her, and he was frowning at her. It wasn't the right time to tell him, she decided. This time when she lifted the brandy glass, she drained it.

"I want our partnership to work," Grant said. "I need it to work for J.D.'s sake. I'm not out to make a quick profit like your last partner. And you have a lot to gain if we remain partners, too. There are advantages for both of us. How about if we forget what happened today and start over? For my part, I'll put more effort into respecting your wishes to keep our relationship strictly business."

He was making perfect sense, Mattie thought, so why did the lump in her throat feel suspiciously like tears?

"Instead of thinking of me as an overprotective brother or a boss, think of me as a friend who can be relied upon for help. Two heads are better than one, and four hands would have been better than two building that brick stairway, don't you think?"

Mattie nodded.

"So we can start over with a clean slate?" Grant extended his hand.

Mattie was just reaching for it when Carlotta's laugh filled the room. "I hope I'm interrupting something."

7

"I DON'T MAKE A HABIT of barging in—" Carlotta waved a hand "—but the door swung open the moment I set foot on the porch. Nice touch, by the way." She let her gaze sweep the foyer. "And the music, it's a harpsichord, isn't it? I like it. It creates a certain mood." She gave Mattie a curious look as she stepped into the parlor. "How did you ever think of it?"

Mattie nearly laughed at the expression on Grant's face. Rising, she drew Carlotta with her into the dining room. "C'mon, I'll show you. I found it in the attic."

One look at the keys playing by themselves had Carlotta glancing back at Mattie. "It's not a player mechanism, is it?" Just to be sure, she knelt down and felt underneath the keyboard. When she stood up, she waved her hand through the air over the bench. "Lordy! All these years I've heard talk about the ghost that haunted this house. But this—" she flashed a grin at Mattie "—child, I'm getting worried now. How am I supposed to compete with a ghost who plays music to entertain the customers?"

"She usually doesn't play for them." Mattie shot a narrow-eyed look at the harpsichord. "Usually, she's very good because she doesn't want to scare the guests away and she lets Lily Clemson do the performing."

There followed a series of arpeggios ending in a trill that sounded suspiciously like a laugh.

"Apparently, she only reveals herself to people who are friends of Mattie's," Grant said.

"You don't suppose she might want a second gig at my place?" Carlotta asked with a laugh. "Only kidding." She winked at Mattie. "And I'm teasing about being bothered by the competition, too. The way I figure it, the more tricks we've got to lure city people out here to the country for a night or two, the more customers we'll all have to share. Once the two of you've got that old mansion spiffed up and running, some of your guests might want a little change of pace and you can send them to the Shallow Creek Inn for dinner." She sent an amused glance at the harpsichord. "And if I get anyone I'd like to see really spooked, I'll send them over here. Sound fair?"

Mattie barely had time to nod before Carlotta was tapping one of her fingers against her forehead. "Which reminds me of why I barged in on you two." As she led the way out of the dining room, Carlotta dug into her fishnet bag. "I have to write everything down now. Then I have to try and remember where I put my notes. Here it is." In the foyer, she paused to unfold the sheet of paper that held Mattie's sketch of the locket. "My gran recognized that locket you described. Not from this drawing, though. By the time I showed it to her, Sheriff Delaney had already dropped by with the real thing. It belonged to Rachel Williams, a young girl who worked in the kitchen two summers."

"Rachel Williams? Lily Clemson told me that there were rumors Peter Barclay was in love with her before he met Mattie Whittaker," Mattie said.

"That would go along with what Gran remembered. She said that Rachel claimed the locket was an engagement gift from Peter, but she couldn't wear it until he told his parents. Then he was called away to fight in the war, and Rachel left town."

"She never came back?" Mattie asked.

Carlotta shook her head. "Gran told the sheriff that there were rumors she had to go away to have a baby. But some believed that Peter Barclay broke her heart, and she went away to forget."

"What about the sapphire ring?" Grant asked.

"Oh, that was your great-aunt's engagement ring. Martha Bickle called this morning to tell me that the ring that was dug up with the bones in the old Barclay mansion definitely belonged to Mattie Whittaker. If Martha's got that piece of news, so does everyone else in a twenty-mile radius." Carlotta folded the sketch and stuffed it back into her bag. Just as she did, the front door swung open. "On second thought, maybe I should worry about the competition." Then she grinned at Mattie. "I didn't breathe a word to Martha Bickle about the locket. The sheriff asked Gran to keep quiet about it. That's why I came in person. I've always suspected Martha of tapping phone lines."

As she stepped off the porch, a gray car turned up the driveway. "A ghost, two skeletons, and you've got a customer on a day you're not even open for business!"

"He's not a customer. That's Pete Desmond from the Merchant's Trust Bank. He represents Amelia Barclay," Grant said as he stepped out on the porch to stand beside Mattie.

"He's a regular customer of mine," Carlotta told them. "And a generous tipper." With a friendly wave, Carlotta hurried across the lawn.

Grant leaned against the railing as Pete Desmond approached. "We're on our way out, Pete."

"I won't keep you, I promise. And I apologize for bothering you again, but I have a favor—"

"We haven't changed our minds about selling to Miss Barclay."

"No, that isn't what I've come about. When I got back to the bank, I had a message to call her. She's coming up here on Friday, and she'd like to meet with you." He saw the refusal in Grant's eyes and switched his attention to Mattie. "She's an old lady, in her seventies, and she's very worried about the scandal now that those skeletons have been discovered."

"Are you saying that the Barclays had something to do with the murders?" Grant asked.

"No. No, of course not. How could anyone even think that? They haven't even owned the place for years."

"The chances are good that the bodies were buried in the cellar while the Barclays were still coming up here for the summers," Grant said.

"I'd be obliged if you wouldn't mention that to her." Pete pulled out a handkerchief and patted his forehead. He didn't succeed in wiping the worry lines away. "She's already upset enough."

"Just how did she find out about it?" Grant asked.

"I told her," Pete said. "She was very close to her brother, and now to have all the scandal dug up again. All I'm asking is that you see her, tell her about your plans. You might be able to reassure her, give her some peace of mind."

"Of course we will," Mattie said before Grant could speak. "Early afternoon around two would be best, after Grant is done at the diner and before things get too hectic around here."

"Thank you." Pete backed up two steps before turning. "Thank you very much."

"Desmond." Grant fell into step beside the banker. "You're certainly going the extra mile for Miss Barclay. Do all of your customers get this kind of personal service?"

Pete turned when he reached his car. "No. I was raised not too far from here, and I owe my college education to the Barclays. They set up a scholarship at the Barclayville Elementary School, and Miss Amelia likes to keep track of the recipients, do business with them if she can. This is the least I can do to repay her family's generosity."

Mattie didn't speak until the gray car had backed its way out onto the road. "You were rude to him again."

"I don't trust him."

"Why not?"

"Maybe because he was hanging around this morning when you got locked in the cellar. And I don't believe that story about the scholarship, either. George had me literally beating the bushes looking for financial aid when I wanted to go to Cornell. I didn't find any scholarship established by the Barclay family."

Mattie thought for a minute. "He graduated about twenty years ahead of you. Ada Mae might know something."

Grant smiled. "A brilliant idea. See? What did I tell you about two heads being better than one? After you, partner." With a bow, he gestured toward his motorcycle.

Mattie frowned. "I don't—"

He grinned at her. "Your choice. But it's air-conditioned. Your car's not."

Mattie reached for the helmet.

THE CLEMSON SISTERS lived in a tidy, picture-book farmhouse, painted dark green with white trim and nestled in the shade of a gnarled old elm tree. The wood on the nearby barn had weathered to a dark gray, but a newly painted white picket fence marked the boundaries of a good-size garden. In its center, a tall scarecrow stood sentinel, its purple chiffon scarf rippling in the breeze.

The moment Grant parked the motorcycle in the driveway, Mattie hopped off and stamped her feet a few times. She wasn't at all sure that the coolness of the ride compensated for the fact that she felt numb from the waist down.

"Problem?" Grant asked.

"Nothing I can't handle," Mattie replied as she turned to lead the way across the grass.

Ada Mae got up from the pansy patch she was weeding and frowned at Grant and Mattie. "You're putting your life at risk riding one of those things."

"Is that any way to greet guests?" Lily unfolded herself from a wicker chair. "Come on up here on the porch where it's cooler. We've been expecting you."

"Hmmph!" Ada Mae snorted as she tossed down her gardening gloves and led the way up the steps. "*She* was expecting you. Had some kind of message when she was playing with those tarot cards of hers!" She shot her sister a frown before she disappeared through the screen door. "I'll get the lemonade."

"Don't pay any attention to her." Lily waved them toward the porch swing. "Ada Mae's been a terrible grouch ever since the sheriff stopped by last evening. She was rude to him, too. The moment he showed her that sapphire ring, she up and announced she was going to bed. When it was still light out!"

Lily plucked a napkin off a plate of brownies and offered them to Grant, smiling when he took one. "But that nice Mr. Delaney didn't take offense. Of course, I told him that she'd had a bit too much sun." Setting the brownies down next to Mattie, Lily arranged herself on the chaise longue. "And he was pleased as punch when I asked him if I could read the cards for him. I didn't know what else to do, what with Ada Mae running off like that. It's been a long time since I've entertained a gentleman. Or done a reading, for that matter. I didn't even know that I had a psychic gift until I married my second husband." Lily paused to fan herself. "Or was it my third?"

Ada Mae pushed through the screen door and began to distribute lemonade. "Thinks she can see into the future! It's just the past that gives her a little trouble."

Lily's eyes fluttered closed as she continued to fan herself. "Sheriff Delaney asked me about the past, too. That locket. I felt such sadness." She placed her hands over her ears. "I can still hear the crying."

"It's over and done with!" Ada Mae set her glass down on the table and turned to Mattie and Grant. "Why can't you just leave it alone?"

"Don't you think that a murderer should pay for his or her crimes?" Mattie asked.

"We don't know that it was murder," Ada Mae insisted.

"It's hard to believe that two women got themselves bricked up in that fireplace by accident," Mattie said.

Ada Mae stared at her.

Lily rose to a sitting position. "Two?"

"Didn't Delaney tell you they found two bodies?" Grant asked.

"It doesn't matter," Ada Mae said. "It's just all the more reason to stop right now before anyone else gets hurt. You tell them what else you saw in those cards, Lily. Tell them." Turning on her heel, Ada Mae disappeared into the house.

"Oh, my." Lily sighed. "She's really upset. Ordinarily, she doesn't have any faith in my ability to read tarot cards."

"What exactly did you see?" Grant asked.

Lily fluttered her hands. "I don't exactly *see*. My gift is not clairvoyance. I'm clairaudient. I hear things. If Ada Mae were here, she'd say it was because I've spent most of my life with my eyes closed." Lily rose. "I really should go to her."

"First, please tell us what you heard," Mattie said.

Lily raised her hands and then dropped them. "Sheriff Delaney asked the cards about the two of you and your plans for the Barclay mansion. That was after he asked about the locket. I heard a sound then. It was very loud."

"What?" Grant asked.

When her eyes met his they were troubled. "Gunshots."

Lily's hand was on the door when Mattie's covered it. "One more thing. You said that Ada Mae was shocked when the sheriff showed her the sapphire ring. When Mattie Whittaker disappeared, didn't anyone suspect foul play?"

"No. Why would we? There were all those letters she sent to George. Oh, my. That's why. . . I have to go to her."

When Lily was gone, Mattie turned to Grant. "I don't like this."

"Two homicides and now gunshots! What's to like?" Grabbing her arm, Grant hurried her toward the bike.

"We're going to have to go see him," Mattie said as she snapped the helmet strap under her chin.

"Don't worry. We're going to get to the bottom of this. Delaney's office is on our way home."

It was a fast ride. Under other circumstances, Mattie might have enjoyed it, but her mind was racing as hard as Grant was pushing the bike. He'd misunderstood her. She'd meant that they had to talk to George Schuler, not Mac Delaney. But the wind that whipped her breath away prevented any discussion.

A sudden burst of speed had her wiggling closer to Grant. Maybe he had purposely misinterpreted what she'd said. George Schuler was the only father he'd ever known. Grant's first instinct would be to protect him. She thought then of Grant's expression just before he'd lowered his visor. Bleak.

And she had no one but herself to blame. She remembered his first reaction to her plan to ferret out the truth. He hadn't wanted any part of it. After all, Grant Whittaker had the best reason in the world to concentrate on the present and the future. His son. She was the only one who felt an obligation to set something right that had happened fifty years ago.

George Schuler was alive and breathing, and he'd taken Grant in and raised him. Mattie Whittaker was dead. Nothing she did would change that.

A sudden jolt from behind scattered her thoughts and sent her ramming into Grant. As the bike fishtailed and the tires squealed on the asphalt, Mattie held on for dear life. Only when they were steady did she dare to glance back. If terror, pure and sharp, hadn't blocked her throat, she would have screamed.

The car was only a few feet away. A quick kaleidoscope of images burned themselves into her brain. She closed her eyes and pictured them more clearly. The hood ornament was a fancy-looking star, and the car was black. She'd seen numbers, GS5 and a T or a 7. Opening her eyes, she risked another look.

She didn't have to turn her head. The car was inching its way alongside them, so close she could have reached out and touched the fender. It was a long car. A limo. It suddenly swerved toward them.

Grant's fingers dug into the handlebars. Gravel spit from beneath the bike as he edged it onto the shoulder. The motorcycle skidded, and he leaned low over the handlebars, praying that Mattie would follow his lead. For a few breathless seconds, the wheels spun. The instant they caught, the bike shot forward.

His eyes riveted on the road, Grant listened, straining to hear the car. For endless minutes, the two vehicles raced side by side in a dead heat. They crested a gentle slope, and Grant saw the guardrail, a blur of white posts bearing down on them. If they were caught between the rail and the car . . .

Grant opened the throttle and the bike sprang ahead. At the last possible moment, he jerked the handlebars to the left and sent the bike flying onto the asphalt. When the wheels slammed down, the motorcycle tilted crazily, and for a moment he thought it would spill them onto the pavement as the tires fought for traction. Then they were upright and racing forward. The screech of metal grazing concrete behind him gave him some satisfaction.

Mattie held tight and prayed. But there wasn't time for even a quick breath of relief before the car hit them again. The bike fishtailed, steadied and roared ahead. Even blurred, the yellow sign with the S-shaped squiggle cautioned a slower speed.

Once more, Grant used all his powers of concentration to keep the bike upright. The road sloped steeply downhill. The curves were sharp, but the guardrails bordering the highway would work in his favor. He swerved in an uneven pattern from one side of the road to the other, banking on the fact that the car would have to cut its speed to stay in control.

While he had a few seconds to think, Grant considered his options. Their only chance was to make the driver of the car believe he had succeeded in running them off the road. As the highway flattened and straightened into a long narrow ribbon in front of him, he tried to picture what lay ahead. There was a farmhouse in about a quarter of a mile. Even above the roar of the bike, he could hear the sudden acceleration of the car behind him, and he braced himself for the impact. When it came, it took all his focus to keep the bike steady.

The farmhouse came into view, and Grant edged the bike onto the shoulder, waiting for the car to move alongside. It was their only choice. Stalling for time, he moved closer and closer to the grass that marked the falloff into a drainage ditch. There was no way to warn Mattie of his plan. Ten yards from the house, he pulled hard on the handlebars and leaned into the turn.

The noise of the motorcycle as it went into a wild spin was deafening. Mattie knew with certainty that she was going to die. She smelled rubber and felt the sting of gravel just before she flew free of the bike. She landed on her arm and felt the breath leave her body as she began to roll.

When she finally came to a stop, she felt as though a mule had kicked her in the stomach. The ground was hard. Luke-warm water was seeping into her clothes. She dragged in a breath and smelled the rank odor of decaying vegetation. Her arm throbbed like a jackhammer when she leaned on it to lever herself up. Wonderful. She was alive. Grant.

She spotted him sitting on the ground rubbing his shoulder. She felt the sting of tears and blinked them back. He was alive. Safe. Tearing her helmet off, she ran toward him.

Rising, Grant pulled her close, running his hands over her. "Are you hurt? Anywhere at all?" He framed her face with his hands.

"My arm. A bruise." She reached up to grip his wrists. "Your shoulder?"

"It'll be fine." For a moment, he just held her. "We're both fine."

Mattie rested her cheek against his chest and let out a long breath. The strong steady beat of his heart pushed away the image of the black car. His sigh seemed to echo her relief. And more. Something warm and soothing was moving through her. Wrapping her arms around him, she held tight.

For just a moment, Grant needed her like this. In his arms. Over her shoulder he could see his bike where it lay on the ground. If it had been a smaller, lighter model, they wouldn't have been so lucky. He pictured the black car speeding away, thinking he should go to the farmhouse, call Mac Delaney. Precious moments were being lost. But he didn't want to let Mattie go. Not yet.

It was Mattie who drew away first, to look at the road. "The limo . . ."

"A limo? You're sure?"

Mattie nodded. "And I saw part of the license plate. GS5 and a T or a 7." She glanced at the motorcycle, then away.

"We're not taking the bike," Grant said as he took her hand and started across the field. "They'll have a phone at the house. We'll call Mac and have him pick us up."

MATTIE SAT with her feet tucked beneath her on the sofa and sipped her wine. The last rays of the sun were slanting through the window and glinting off the beer bottle that Mac Delaney was using to make a point to Grant.

In addition to writing up a detailed report of the accident and alerting the state police, the local sheriff had also played chauffeur, delivering them home to Whittaker House. Then he'd shifted quite comfortably into the role of mother hen, bribing one of his deputies to deliver a pizza while she and Grant cleaned up after their dip in the ditch.

It had taken only one whiff of the spicy sauce to alert Mattie to the fact that she was starving. Now she was stuffed.

"I still say we lost the game when Eddie Cashman missed that fly ball in the top of the sixth," Grant said.

Mattie studied them over the rim of her glass as Mac launched into a rebuttal. Men were so different from women. Of course, she'd known that for a very long time, but it never hurt to have an old belief reinforced. The two men had been talking baseball ever since they'd dug into the pizza. Not about the sport in general, but about one very specific game from their long ago and, she was sure, misspent youth. How could it matter after all these years who had made the fatal error that had cost Barclayville the championship?

Mattie took another sip of wine and realized that she was very relaxed. Seated next to Grant and listening to a conversation so far removed from that mad ride they had taken on his motorcycle made her feel so...ordinary. So at home. She was suddenly overtaken by a yawn.

"Now, I can take a hint." Mac shot her a grin as he set his bottle on the table and unfolded himself from the couch.

Grant rose with him. "You'll keep in touch? Let us know when you find out who was driving that car?"

"You bet." Mac frowned as the front door swung open at his approach. "Get this lock fixed."

Grant shot the dead bolt and strode back into the parlor. "Delaney isn't going to tell us a thing if he traces that plate."

"He made it pretty clear in his office that he doesn't want us to investigate on our own."

"He might have a point." Grant's gaze dropped to Mattie's arm where a bruise was already forming. He moved toward her then as the anger and fear rolled through him. "Mattie, I—"

"No." She raised a hand. "I know what you're going to say. That maybe Ada Mae is right and we ought to let the dead rest in peace. All I've been able to think about is your great-aunt and that other poor girl. I hadn't really thought it through—or at least—" She lifted her hands and dropped them. "I didn't think about other people."

"What are you trying to say?" Grant asked.

Mattie reached for her wine and took another sip. "I've only looked at this whole thing from my point of view. Bringing the murderer to justice and lifting the curse."

"And what's the other point of view?" Grant asked.

"Whoever murdered those women might be somebody we know."

"Wait." Grant shook his head. "Are you saying that you've changed your mind? You don't want to see justice done?"

Mattie's chin lifted. "Well, *you* didn't want to at first."

"That was before. I didn't much care about two women who were killed fifty years ago. But I sure as hell care when somebody tries to kill you and me. And if I get my hands on the creep who locked you in the cellar—"

"What if it's someone you know?" Mattie asked.

"Then they're going to be very sorry they know me." Grant studied her for a minute, then grabbed a pad of paper and a pencil from the bar and handed it to her. "Who do you suspect, Mattie?" He sat across from her on the opposite sofa. "Why don't we make a list?"

Mattie crossed her legs beneath her, and rested the pad on her knee. When she hesitated, tapping the pencil on the paper, Grant said, "Delaney is trying to trace Rachel Williams and find out if she had a baby. Even if he succeeds, I think we can eliminate the child as a suspect. He or she would have been much too young."

"But they might have a reason for hiding the truth."

"Then they'd be protecting the person who murdered their mother," Grant said.

"They might not know that. Who knows what lies they might have been told? Little children are like clean slates. You can tell them anything. They're a perfect way to rewrite history."

"Okay," Grant said. "Put Rachel Williams's child on the list with a question mark since we're not sure if he or she exists."

Mattie began to write. "Then there's Ada Mae and Lily."

"Good grief! You don't suspect them?"

Mattie looked at him. "Ada Mae was dead set against my plan to expand into the Barclay mansion from the very first, and Lily thought the vibrations were bad."

"They were worried about the curse," Grant said. "Ada Mae's never married, and Lily's had how many husbands?"

"Seven, I think. But they also knew we were on that road."

"And where did they get the limo? Do you think they keep one stashed in the barn?"

Mattie met his eyes squarely. "I think we have to consider all possible suspects."

"Then put George Schuler's name as number three."

"You're sure?" Mattie asked.

"Is this what's been bothering you?" Grant asked. "I don't believe for a moment that George had anything to do with murdering those two women. He'd never hurt anyone. The Clemson sisters, either. But George and Ada Mae have been close friends ever since I can remember, and it's pretty clear that she's worried about him."

"Lily claims it's more than friendship. She says Ada Mae's been sweet on George for years, but George has never stopped carrying the torch for Mattie." Mattie paused for a second and frowned. "Which doesn't make any sense at all if he knew she was dead." She pointed her pencil at Grant. "And he couldn't have been driving that limo. Unless he has an accomplice."

"And that brings us right back to the Clemson sisters tooling around old country roads in a black limo," Grant said with a grin. "I'm having a great deal of trouble picturing those two old ladies involved in any of this. We better have a talk with George tomorrow. Maybe he can shed some light on the problem, or at least speak up in his own defense." Grant leaned forward. "In the meantime, I'd much rather pin something on Pete Desmond. Put him down as number four."

"The banker?" Mattie asked. "He's too young. He didn't have means, method or opportunity."

"He had all three on the day you got locked in the cellar of the Barclay mansion. That's enough for me. And while you're at it, add Amelia Barclay to your list. The Barclays owned the house fifty years ago."

After adding the names, Mattie frowned at the list. "We don't have one piece of solid evidence to link any of these people to the murders. We have to find out who was driving that car today."

Rising, she glanced at her watch, then walked to the phone and punched in numbers. "Mom? I was hoping I'd get you.

Sure." Placing her hand over the receiver, she said to Grant, "She's going to pick up in her office. My sister-in-law, C.J., is a defense attorney. She has contacts on the police force in Syracuse. Maybe she can help." She took her hand off the receiver. "I'm fine, Mom. How's C.J.?"

Grant watched her as she began to pace, talking to her mother. She certainly looked none the worse for wear after her roll into the ditch. Except for the purple bruise that colored her right forearm. Just looking at it made his hands curl into fists.

He got up and walked into the foyer. While Mattie had showered, he and Mac Delaney had argued over how to keep her safe. Mac had suggested that Mattie move in with her family in Syracuse and commute to Barclayville to run her restaurant on the weekends. It was clearly the safest course of action, but Grant knew that Mattie wouldn't even consider it.

His own plan was to keep her at his side and pray that he could protect her. He couldn't afford to let her out of his sight. He leaned his shoulder against the wall, and concentrated on relaxing. The problem was, if he succeeded in keeping her close for the next few days, how in the world was he going to keep his hands off her?

Even now, he couldn't keep his eyes off her hair. Fastened back from her face with a red clip, it fell halfway down her back, and it was still damp from her shower. He could smell it from where he was standing. Vanilla. And some other scent that was uniquely Mattie. The scent had lingered in the air, filling his senses when he had used her bathroom to wash.

She'd changed into a white tank top and shorts which emphasized the length of her slender legs. The kind of legs a man fantasized about in his dreams. He could imagine how smooth they would feel, how tightly they might wrap themselves around him.

She was laughing at something her mother was saying. Grant felt his mouth suddenly go bone-dry.

"No, it's nothing to worry about. A strange car in a small town gets everyone talking, and I thought it might be a good idea to have C.J. check it out. No, I'm not alone. Grant Whittaker has decided to camp out with his dog in the front parlor, just in case. So I have plenty of protection. Yes. Love you, too."

Mattie hung up the phone and crossed her fingers. "Let's hope that works. She has a very special kind of radar for lies, it's like one of those heat-seeking . . ."

Mattie's voice trailed off when she glanced up and met the heat in Grant's eyes. Her heart beating faster, she said, "You're not upset because I told her you were staying here? I was just trying to discourage her from sending my brother up to drag me home."

"You might be safer if he did," Grant said.

Mattie's eyes narrowed. "I thought we settled all that. The *safest* thing we can do is to find out who the murderer is before he or she can strike again."

"I'm not talking about that." He looked at her intently. "I want you, Mattie. I'm not sure how much longer I can keep you safe from me."

Safe. Neither one of them moved. For a moment, the need between them vibrated so intensely Mattie could almost hear it, like a wire pulled taut and about to be struck. She'd known for hours now that she loved him. Perhaps it was time to accept it, and admit that being safe wasn't what she wanted. What she wanted was Grant Whittaker.

She took a step forward. He took a step back. "Where are you going?" she asked.

"I'm taking Hannibal for a walk. A long one."

"Stay."

"Mattie, if I stay now, we're going to make love."

She smiled at him, then took his hand and drew him into the room. "Didn't you tell me we were going to make love on this couch? Many times?" Bracing one leg on the cushion, she began to unbutton his shirt.

"Are you sure?" Grant asked.

"Uh-huh." She unfastened the rest of the buttons.

Grant stopped her hands. "Are you protected?"

Her eyes were smiling as she slid the shirt off his shoulders. "I told you I know how to take care of myself." Placing her hands on his chest, she could see the last rays of the setting sun on his skin and she recalled the first time she'd seen him, lying on the hammock, how much she'd wanted to touch him just like this. The hunger that burned inside of her now had begun then.

She found pleasure, sharp and sweet, in the narrow length of his collarbone and temptation in the pulse that throbbed near his throat. It was as if his body had been designed to suit her ultimate fantasy. Everything delighted her—the corded muscles of his arms, the leanness of his waist.

Her hands felt so cool on his skin, in odd contrast to the little licks of fire that her touch sent dancing along his nerve endings. His own hands seemed to move of their own volition to touch her hair. How often had he thought of doing this? He undid the clip, then carefully threaded his fingers through the soft silk until his hands were trapped.

"Kiss me," she whispered, pressing her fingers against the back of his neck to draw him closer. "No one's ever made me feel the way you do when you kiss me."

Grant felt the pleasure arrow sharp and stunning as he brushed his lips against hers. He only meant to sample, to savor her taste. But she was so moist, her flavor so sweet and addictive. Resisting her was no more possible than preventing himself from taking his next breath.

As Grant deepened the kiss, she felt the heat, the threat, the promise. Each sensation was so clear. The calluses on his fingers as he pushed down the straps of her tank top, the softness of the sofa sinking beneath their combined weights as they knelt torso to torso. There was music, soft with an insistent rhythm, but Mattie heard only Grant's ragged breathing, her own rapid heartbeat as she ran her hands up his back.

So this is what it meant to be consumed, she thought as he began to explore every part of her. His mouth lingered beneath her breast as he unsnapped her shorts. Then, as he tugged them off, he shifted her so that she was trapped between the back of the couch and his body.

His lips nibbled at hers as he toyed with the thin silk of her panties. His fingers skimmed lace from where it rose high along her thighs to where it disappeared between her legs, then they slipped beneath to find her moist heat.

Madness, Mattie thought as he sent her spinning with only his touch into a world of sensations. Heat. She was burning with it. She couldn't seem to get enough as she arched against his hand. She was aware of the ridges of the cushions at her back, the hardness of his body. She couldn't seem to move, but couldn't keep from trembling as her body arched again and again.

As his fingers probed deeper, Grant watched her eyes widen, then cloud. He couldn't have described the feelings that poured through him to hear the way her breath caught then released on his name, to feel the way her body strained against his as passion overtook her.

Dazed, floating, Mattie wasn't sure she would ever have the energy to move again. There wouldn't be any need to if only Grant would go on holding her this way. But when he tried to draw away, she went with him. Her hands were as desperate as his in the struggle to get rid of his jeans. As she tugged and wiggled them down his legs, her own hunger began to grow again.

Her mouth was as demanding as his, her greed as consuming. She savored his taste, darker at his neck where his pulse beat so frantically, deeper, more male at his waist. Then she was pulling him with her onto the cushions.

He'd seen them like this, Grant recalled when she was beneath him, her legs wrapped around him. They'd been naked, tangled on the love seat with a fire licking at the logs behind them. But they didn't need the fire. The flames were in him, in her. And they grew higher, hotter, as he drove himself into her.

Then there was only Mattie. She was all he could see, all he could feel as they began to move together, no longer able to control their craving for that final flash of delight.

There was only Grant, Mattie thought as she held him tight, and gave herself over to the roar of the wind, the burst of pleasure.

"Only you." She breathed and, then, as one, they shuddered in an explosion of ecstasy.

8

THE CAR was absolutely stifling. What little air blew through the open windows provided no relief. Mattie tried to concentrate on the scenery and relax. She caught a glimpse of sun glinting off a winding stream as the car bumped its way over a bridge. The water would be cool, a welcome relief to the oppressing heat in the car. Her thoughts returned once more to Grant, who hadn't said a word to her since they'd started driving. A couple of explanations for his silence had occurred to her. First, he hadn't liked leaving her alone when he'd left for the diner, but he'd accepted the logic of her argument that since it was Thursday, she had desserts to prepare for her guests tonight.

Or maybe he was just tired. The night had been . . . she wasn't even sure there was a word to describe it. They'd woken up late and he'd had to rush off to the diner so they hadn't talked about what had happened between them. Maybe it was too soon. After all, it had happened so fast. How long had they known each other. A week? And maybe in Grant's mind, there was nothing to discuss. His approach to life seemed so easy and casual.

She looked at him then, studying his profile. The strength she saw only enhanced his good looks. She'd known that first day that he wasn't as laid-back and aimless as he appeared. Beneath that humor and teasing charm, Grant Whittaker was a man with goals that were important to him. She recalled her conversation with J.D. about security. Grant was a man who could be counted on to provide it.

He'd made it clear to her from the beginning that his son came first. She admired him for that. And he'd made it equally clear that he wanted her. So he couldn't be having regrets, could he?

No. There were a million explanations for his abstraction—like two murders, threats against her, an attempt on their lives and the fact that they were now going to interrogate the man who'd been like a father to him.

Mattie thought of her own father and her heart twisted. If George was involved in what had happened to Mattie Whittaker . . .

"Harrison House is just beyond the trees," Grant said as he turned the car onto a winding, graveled drive.

On the top of the hill sat the nursing home, a red-brick building with white pillars, shaded by ancient elm trees. The moment the car stopped, Mattie got out, then waited for Grant to climb over the gearshift. When he straightened beside her, she said, "It's not too late."

"Too late for what?"

Though his voice was calm, Mattie could read a different message in his eyes. She took a deep breath. "Maybe it was a mistake—"

"A mistake?" The storm in his eyes grew more intense. "I didn't think you were a quitter."

"I'm not."

"Good. Because there's no going back for us. If you're having any regrets, forget them. What happened between us last night is just the beginning."

Mattie heard exactly what he was saying, and what he wasn't. But she could also hear music in her head, a tune the harpsichord played all the time. She smiled. "Okay. But I wasn't talking about us, I was talking about George. Are you up to seeing him?"

Taking her arm, Grant urged her up the path. "Of course. I told you before. I'm not worried."

As they walked past the white pillars and checked in at the administration office, Mattie wished she felt as confident. An aide led them to the back porch and pointed to one of the walks that wound its way through the grounds saying, "George usually takes his exercise over by the hedge before lunch. He's quite faithful about it."

A lush, green hedge, some distance off, bordered the property as far as Mattie could see. Beyond it, the earth fell away into a wide, deep valley with mist still clinging to it in patches. As she and Grant walked along the path, they passed a group of ladies playing cards in the shade of a gazebo. Other residents were walking, some were being pushed in wheelchairs and a few sat on benches arranged strategically in shady areas.

"Nice place," Mattie said.

"George can't wait to get out. That's why he's so faithful about his exercise. Running the diner has kept him in pretty good shape for a man of seventy-five. The doctors say he'll be back in Barclayville by the end of the summer."

Mattie spotted George moving his walker at a steady pace along the paved walkway next to the hedge. He looked a little more frail than when he'd taken her on a tour of Whittaker House a year ago, but he moved with confidence, and the blue eyes behind the thick wire-rimmed glasses were as alert as ever.

"Sit. Sit." George waved them to a brightly painted green bench under a tree. "Ada Mae was here last night. She said you might stop by." Mattie lowered herself to the grass, leaving room for Grant next to George.

While the two men chatted about the diner, Mattie tried to gather her thoughts. Grant had to be right. She found it impossible to believe that the man sitting in front of her in the bright sunlight was a murderer.

George elbowed Grant. "We're boring a lovely woman with shoptalk. Unforgivable." Resting one arm along the top of his walker, George pointed out over the hedge. "You see that cut in the hills over there that runs at a right angle to the valley? That's what they call a hanging valley. It was left behind by a melting glacier near the end of the Ice Age. A lot of the terrain in upstate New York was formed by glaciers." He shifted his gaze from Mattie to Grant. "But I don't think you came here today for a lecture on earth science. Ada Mae tells me that Hannibal dug up a skeleton in the old fireplace at the Barclay mansion. And you think it's Mattie Whittaker's."

"Did she tell you about the sapphire ring?" Mattie asked. "Even Martha Bickle's sure it's Mattie Whittaker's."

George's breath came out on a sigh as he looked out over the valley again. "The old mansion was bound to give up its secret sooner or later. Maybe now, everyone in Barclayville can have some peace."

"We're not going to have any peace," Grant said, "not until we find out who killed those two women fifty years ago and who's trying to get rid of Mattie right now."

"Two?" George looked first at Mattie, then at Grant. "Someone's made a mistake."

"The medical examiner's report says two skeletons. Two women in their late teens, early twenties. One was bricked up behind the other, and they both died of broken necks."

"Two." George repeated and shook his head. "I don't understand. And you say that someone's trying to hurt Mattie?"

Grant went on to explain about the phone call, the anonymous note, Mattie's ordeal in the cellar and the motorcycle ride. George just kept shaking his head. "It doesn't make any sense. There's no reason for either of you to be in any danger." Gripping the handles of his walker, he started to stand, then suddenly sank back down. "Two. That would explain . . ."

"Explain what?" Grant asked.

"Why the bricks at the back of the fireplace were a lighter shade. It's funny the tricks your mind plays. Why would that little detail stay with me when I've tried so hard to forget everything that happened that night. Sometimes, I even succeeded in convincing myself that it was something I dreamed, a horrible nightmare that never really happened. But I remember that the bricks at the back of the fireplace were a lighter color." George turned to look at Grant. "I should have told you a long time ago. I'm responsible for Mattie Whittaker's death as surely as if I'd pushed her down those stairs."

"You didn't kill her," Grant said, reaching over to cover one of George's hands with his.

For a moment, George didn't speak. Then he cleared his throat. "Thank you for that. I didn't push her. That part was an accident. She fell. I was there in the foyer. I saw her running down the hall along the balustrade. And then when she reached the top of the stairs, she tripped." George lifted his free hand from the walker. "I can still see the way she reached out, trying to grab on to something, anything. Maybe if she hadn't been running, but the momentum . . . and there was nothing for her to grab but air. She pitched forward and rolled over and over until she reached the bottom of the stairs. I knew she was dead even before Miss Barclay took her pulse." He dropped his fisted hand into his lap.

"Amelia Barclay was there that night?" Mattie asked.

George nodded. "It was two days before the wedding. She'd offered to drive Mattie back up here. Told me Mattie got a disturbing letter and had to come back to check it out. Then Mattie found something that upset her on the third floor in one of the servant's rooms. Amelia said she ran out crying. And then she tripped . . . I'm the person who wrote the letter that brought them back to the mansion. If I hadn't sent it, Mattie Whittaker might be alive today."

For a moment, they sat in silence broken only by the occasional trill of a bird, the drone of insects.

When George spoke again, he was looking out over the valley. "I was fifteen and in love for the first time. A true case of puppy love. Mattie never even knew how I felt until two weeks before the wedding when Miss Amelia came to drive her back to Manhattan. I got up the courage to give her flowers that morning. She was kind. She touched my cheek and thanked me. I can still remember how cool her hand felt. You don't know how often I've wished that that had been the end of the story."

Grant tightened his grip on George's hand. "What happened?"

"I got a letter in the mail from a Rachel Williams. I remembered her. She lived over near Mason's Corners, and she was a few years ahead of the Clemson sisters and me in school. In the letter, she claimed that she had borne Peter Barclay's son and that he had promised to marry her. But then Peter had been called away to fight in the war and had changed his mind and denied the boy was his when he came back. But Rachel claimed she had proof. She'd hidden something in her room at the Barclay mansion. It was under a loose board at the head of the bed. And anyone who cared for Mattie Whittaker would let her know."

George paused to look from Mattie to Grant. "I thought I was doing the right thing when I sent that letter. I didn't mean to cause her death. But I was a coward when I agreed to brick her up in that fireplace."

"Why did you do it?" Grant asked.

"Miss Amelia pleaded with me, told me that it was going to be hard enough on her brother, as it was. He was running for the state senate. If there was a scandal, it might ruin his chances in the upcoming election. Wasn't it bad enough that he'd lost his future wife? And she pointed out that I had my own future to think about. That if we called in the authorities, they might not take our word for what happened. So I carried your great-aunt down into that cellar and helped brick her up. I even went along with it later when Miss Amelia wrote those letters. I pretended that they came from Mattie Whittaker. I've kept the secret ever since. I never told anyone what happened that night." He turned to Grant. "I should have told you. But when you first came to live with me, you were only ten. I told myself you were too young. Then when you got older, I couldn't tell you. I was afraid you'd never forgive me."

Grant put his arms around the older man and simply held him. "You were only fifteen. There's nothing to forgive."

As Mattie watched the two men, she wasn't even aware of her tears until one of them dropped on her hand. She wiped them away while she watched Grant pat the older man's shoulder. It was a gesture she'd seen him use with J.D. Then, Grant was helping George to his feet, and she rose to join them as they began walking up the path.

They hadn't gone more than a few steps before she said, "You know, we've been assuming that the other skeleton belonged to Rachel Williams. Carlotta Strong's grandmother identified the locket that was found with the remains as the one Rachel had shown to her friends, claiming it was an engagement gift from Peter Barclay."

George frowned. "But the letter was signed by Rachel."

"Someone else could have written it," Mattie said.

"I suppose. But Mattie Whittaker was holding a locket in her hand when I put her in the fireplace. I remember Miss Amelia tried to pry her fingers loose from the chain, but she couldn't. Couldn't break it, either. Later, I wondered if the locket was what she'd found under that floorboard."

"So the locket was buried with Mattie and not the other woman." Mattie frowned. "If the other skeleton isn't Rachel Williams, who is it?"

"Mr. Schuler, you're a very popular man lately." A nurse hurried toward them. "A visitor on Tuesday, two this morning and now a special gift basket." She handed him a wicker basket wrapped in cellophane and filled with colorfully wrapped boxes. "I shouldn't give it to you before lunch, but you eat like a bird, anyway. This will put some meat on your bones."

George frowned at her. "The food here's lousy. If you'd let me loose in that kitchen, just for one meal, you'd have a revolution on your hands."

The nurse smiled, and Mattie could tell this was a conversation they'd had more than once.

"Threats," the nurse said. "That's all we get from you." She turned to Mattie and Grant. "We've offered to let him cook, but then he claims he's a resident here. Says he's on vacation." She shifted her gaze to George. "Instead of complaining, you can enjoy these fancy cookies and cakes."

"I don't want it."

"Maybe it's from Ada Mae," Mattie said.

George peered through the cellophane. "She'd never send me Italian biscotti or petit fours. She knows I like my food plain, not fancy. So does everyone in Barclayville."

Mattie glanced at Grant and nearly grinned at the bland look he gave her in return.

"I could put it in the staff room," the nurse offered. "They'll eat anything. Miniature pecan tortes. They'll think they've died and gone to heaven."

"No. There's enough people around here about to cash in their chips without the staff doing it, too," George said as he handed the basket to Mattie. "I'd like you to have it. Thanks to you, the both of you, I've lightened my conscience a great deal today."

"Does Ada Mae know what you've told us?"

George shook his head.

"Tell her," Mattie said. "She'll understand. Mattie Whittaker does." She gave George a hug before she and Grant left him arguing with the nurse about something.

"POOR MAN," Mattie said as they climbed into the car with the basket. "He was too young to have to deal with the guilt and the grief." Even as she said it, she recalled her own experience with loss at the age of ten, and Grant's. They drove for a while in silence, both lost in thought.

Mattie was rerunning in her mind everything that George had told them. She knew she should be feeling relieved that Mattie Whittaker hadn't been murdered, but she wasn't. Several things bothered her. She glanced over at Grant and noticed his shoulders were tense, as was his grip on the steering wheel. Evidently he wasn't happy with George's story, either. Perhaps if they talked about it, the whole thing would make more sense.

"You know, if the other skeleton doesn't belong to Rachel Williams, she could still be alive," she ventured.

"It doesn't matter," Grant said.

"Of course it matters. If Rachel Williams is alive, we have to find out who was really bricked up behind Mattie Whittaker. We'll have to call Mac Delaney." Mattie glanced at her watch. It was almost one o'clock. "*You'll* have to call him and fill him in. I still have a dessert to finish."

The car bumped over a wooden bridge. Below it ran a stream. Grant slowed and turned down a dirt road. Mattie didn't even notice. "Maybe we should offer to pay for a private investigator to check dental records. It might speed things up a little. And another thing." She turned to Grant. "George claims that Mattie Whittaker's death was an accident." She raised a hand to emphasize her point. "And I believe that he was telling the truth about what he saw. But what about that other woman? Whoever she is. The medical examiner said that both women died because their necks were broken." Mattie's eyebrows rose. "One accident, okay. But I can't believe that two women tripped and took a header down those stairs."

Grant stopped the car and turned toward her. She was so absorbed in what she was saying, wondering what had happened all those years ago. And all he could picture was a woman falling down stairs, reaching out, clutching at the air. And he was at the bottom of the stairs in the foyer of the Barclay mansion watching helplessly. Like George. Only the woman he saw falling was Mattie Farrell. His Mattie.

Suddenly, Mattie noticed that they had stopped. Grant had parked the car by a stream. When she looked at him, she saw heat in his eyes.

"Mac suggested yesterday that we tell everyone we're postponing our plans for expanding into the Barclay mansion. That we're waiting until he has more time to investigate."

"You can't do that," Mattie said. "It's essential to move quickly, for J.D.'s sake."

Hadn't he already said much the same thing to himself? Lisa's mother was coming to dinner on Sunday. And thanks to Mattie, she was hoping to help them with the renovation of the Barclay mansion. How impressed would she be with his stability as a parent if he suddenly announced that they were postponing their plans?

"Besides," Mattie continued, "we're getting so close. Someone has gotten away with murder for fifty years. The only thing that's brought this person out of the woodwork now is what we're doing at the Barclay mansion. If we quit—"

Grant gripped her shoulders. "You're talking about this as if it were some damned board game. Don't you understand that your life is in danger?"

"What about you? You were on that motorcycle, too."

"But I wasn't locked in the cellar. I wasn't alone in Whittaker House getting threatening phone calls and notes."

Mattie frowned thoughtfully. "You know, maybe this killer has a thing for women. They say that some serial killers murder the same person over and over."

"It doesn't matter," Grant said. The fact that she was right, that everything she said made sense, did nothing to calm the emotions rolling through him. "The only thing that matters is you." If he could convince her of nothing else, he had to convince her of that.

Pulling her close, he covered her mouth with his. He explored her taste with his tongue as if there were some flavor that she would keep from him, but she gave everything.

Even then, he might have maintained control if she hadn't answered his demands with an urgency that matched his own. Impatient with the gearshift that separated them, Grant dragged her closer. He pulled her shirt from her shorts and found the hot, slick silk of her skin. Not even for a second did his mouth leave hers.

A kiss. No one had ever been able to make her feel this needy, this desperate with a kiss. Always before, Mattie had thought of kissing as a prelude. A beginning. But Grant's kisses were madness. They started fires that threatened to consume her. His body was like a furnace. Even through his clothes, she could feel the heat. Tempting. She tried to pull off his shirt. There was no room. Aching to feel his skin beneath her hands, she grabbed his T-shirt and yanked.

The moment he heard the cotton rip, Grant felt his own need tear through him. She wanted as much as he wanted. He could feel it in the scrape of her teeth on his shoulder, the scratch of her nails on his back, in her quick, ragged breaths. Everywhere he touched, he felt her blood pulsing. For him.

Somehow, he found the strength to draw back. Breathless and a little dazed, he looked into her eyes. "I want you. Now."

Her lips curved as she ran her hand over him in one long, possessive stroke. "Yes," she breathed.

Grant lifted her then, settling her back into the passenger seat. His hand searched for and found the lever to collapse it. Then he moved, straddling the gearshift and squeezing himself into the space above her. Arms and legs tangling, they struggled with their clothes. The cramped quarters only increased their desperation.

Mattie tore at the snap of his jeans and drew down his zipper. She heard his moan when her hand found him. Then he threaded his fingers with hers, drawing them away before she dragged him over that last jagged edge.

With one hand, Grant pulled off her shorts and the thin scrap of silk underneath. Even as he shoved down his jeans, she wrapped her legs around him. Grant had wanted before, but not like this. He'd known greed, but it had never sliced him in half. When she would have reached for him again, he trapped her wrist in one hand.

Outside the window of the car, insects droned. Birds trilled. Neither of them noticed.

"I need you."

Afterward, Grant couldn't recall which of them had spoken the words. He drove into her and watched the shock of pleasure cloud her eyes. All he could see was her as he withdrew and pushed in again. When she arched toward him, meeting each of his thrusts, the last of Grant's control snapped and together they raced to a place neither of them had been before.

When he could breathe again, feel again, think, he realized that he had taken her on the front seat of a car like a teenager with raging hormones. She was soft and pliant beneath him. As he levered himself up, he felt her hand slide off him.

Mattie opened her eyes to find him staring down at her. Stunned. It was the only word she could think of to describe the expression on his face. And no wonder. It was exactly how *she* felt.

"Are you okay?" he asked.

"I think so." Aside from the armrest, which felt as if it had been permanently imbedded in her thigh, she felt wonderful. "Maybe after a few months at Harrison House, I'll be able to walk again."

"I'm sorry." He tried to move, but she linked her arms around his neck and her lips curved in a smile.

"I'm fine. Amazing, in fact." She glanced around the interior of the car. "If we managed to make love in the front seat of this car, solving a fifty-year-old murder and lifting a curse is going to be a snap!"

Grant's laughter, rich and deep, filled the car as he rested his forehead against hers. "Only you, Farrell."

"Only you, Whittaker," she said, and brushed her lips against his.

THE MOMENT GRANT stopped the car in the driveway, Mattie hopped out and hurried across the lawn. She had two hours to frost the Black Forest cake. At four o'clock sharp, Ada Mae and Lily would arrive, and then she would have to turn her attention to the rest of tonight's menu.

Grant caught up to her as she reached the porch. Hannibal lay sprawled across the bottom step. Without moving, he whined a sleepy greeting as they stepped over him. Grant reached for Mattie's arm and drew her closer the moment he saw that the door was ajar. Together they approached it, but the door didn't swing open. The harpsichord didn't make a sound. Stepping in front of Mattie, Grant walked into the foyer.

They both saw the envelope on the banister. Mattie went cold all over, and in that one moment when she hesitated, Grant grabbed it.

"Daddy!"

He turned in time to catch J.D., who had launched himself into his father's arms.

All Mattie could think of was how cool and neat Lynda Ackerman looked in her navy silk walking shorts and blouse as she rose from the sofa and walked into the foyer. She was sure that she and Grant looked as though they'd been tossed around and then dropped by a tornado. Mattie didn't dare let her gaze shift to the rip in Grant's T-shirt. Hopefully, J.D. was blocking his grandmother's view.

"You've got a big hole in your shirt," J.D. said.

"Oh." Grant feigned surprise. "I must have caught it on the gearshift climbing out of Mattie's car."

"Forgive us for barging in like this," Lynda said. "I pulled all the way into the back hoping to find your car. We would have waited on the porch, but the door swung right open."

"I'm glad it did," Mattie said. "You and J.D. are welcome here any time."

Lynda gave the door a puzzled frown. "I couldn't get it to shut all the way."

"Was this envelope here when you came in?" Grant asked.

"No. A young man in a pickup dropped it off. Said it was the estimate you asked for on the carpentry work and painting. He can start next Monday." Lynda turned to Mattie. "I know we weren't supposed to come until Sunday, and we won't stay long, but I talked with my daughter last night, and I wanted to speak with Grant."

Grant lowered J.D. to the floor and leaned down so that he was at eye level with his son. "Why don't you go out and see if you can get Hannibal to run around? I think he's been sleeping for almost forty-eight hours."

When J.D. looked up at Mattie, she held out her hand. "C'mon," she said. "This is a two-person job."

Out on the porch, Hannibal was giving a good imitation of being dead. Sitting on the top step, Mattie studied the dog. "I think we're going to need a bomb."

J.D. glanced at her curiously. "A bomb?"

"Lifting him with a crane wouldn't necessarily wake him up." She lifted one of the dog's ears and shouted, "Hannibal!" The eye she'd uncovered didn't even blink. "Want to give it a try?" She offered the ear to J.D.

Squatting, he leaned closer and yelled, "Hannibal!"

The dog didn't so much as quiver.

"What d'ya think?" Mattie asked.

"You got any blueberry buckle?"

Mattie shot him a quick look. His wire-rimmed glasses had slipped low on his nose, and the mischievous laughter, so like his father's, was clear in his eyes. She grinned at him as she pushed his glasses up. "He really ran fast with that basket, didn't he? I never did get it back. But I've got some fancy little cakes and cookies in the car."

Hannibal continued to play dead while she led J.D. across the lawn. The basket had suffered some damage when Grant had collapsed the seat, but she and J.D. still managed to unwrap several uncrushed biscotti and a trio of petit fours. Together, they placed them on the step as close as they could get to Hannibal's nose.

The dog didn't stir.

"I give up," Mattie said. Then she glanced at J.D. "I'd offer you some, but that stuff we left in the car was pretty smooshed."

"S'okay," J.D. said. "I'm not supposed to eat sweets in between meals."

"My mom had a rule like that, too," Mattie said. "That's why I became a chef. Chefs never *eat* anything in between meals. But they have to sample. It's part of the job." She glanced at her watch. "And right now my job is to make chocolate frosting. Would you like to be my assistant?"

At J.D.'s nod, Mattie led the way around the house to the kitchen entrance.

IT WAS THE NOISE that eventually drew Grant and Lynda to the kitchen. It sounded like a war was being waged. In the doorway, Grant put his hand on his ex-mother-in-law's arm and stopped to watch.

Mattie had her arms around J.D. Heads close together, they were squeezing frosting through parchment paper. They looked as though they'd been locked in mortal combat. Chocolate was smeared across the white jackets they were wearing, J.D.'s hair was spiked with it and the refrigerator and one of the walls had been caught in the crossfire.

Grant couldn't identify what he was feeling as he watched Mattie and his son. It was like a punch low in his gut. And he wasn't sure he could speak around the lump in his throat. If this was love, he wasn't falling. He'd been knocked to the floor, and he was pretty sure he was out for the count.

"Bam!" J.D. said as a lump of frosting shot out of the tube of paper and landed on the edge of the cake. Then he giggled. "It looks just like a bullet."

"The recipe calls for little rosettes, but bullets it will have to be," Mattie said, giving the parchment another twist. "There. Try it by yourself."

"Bam! Bam! Bam!" Three more lumps landed on the cake. "Bam!" Mattie caught the last bullet on her arm.

"We can't let it go to waste," she said as she swiped half of it up with her finger and put it in her mouth.

"No," J.D. agreed, following suit.

"What is going on here?" Lynda demanded.

Mattie and J.D. jumped guiltily, then exchanged a quick look before they turned to face their accuser.

"I'm not eating in between meals," J.D. hastened to explain. "Tasting is part of my job." He puffed out his chest. "I'm Mattie's assistant."

"I see," Grant said, struggling to hold back a laugh. "It looks like hard work." He walked toward his son. "Let's get you cleaned up, or your grandmother won't let you in her car."

The instant Mattie had him out of the jacket, J.D. leaped into his father's arms. "A shower!" he demanded.

"It's the only solution," Grant said as he carried the little boy out of the room.

Mattie gestured toward one of the stools that surrounded the work island. "Sit down. I'm about ready for some iced tea."

"I'm sure you have work to do. I can wait outside."

Mattie waved a hand. "I work better with an audience." She gave the cake a narrow-eyed look. "Hopefully."

"You're very good with J.D.," Lynda said as Mattie rinsed her hands and pulled glasses from a cupboard.

Mattie smiled and poured tea. "It's not hard."

"I find him quite a handful. Last night, he let his two gerbils out of their cage. Martin, my butler, is still searching for one of them." Lynda glanced around the kitchen. "Of course, playing with frosting isn't something that I'd think of letting him do, myself. I don't think I even allowed Lisa in the kitchen when she was little. I thought it was important for a little girl to be clean and neat. That's the way I was raised." She glanced at the cake. "We may have missed out on a lot of fun."

Mattie put the pitcher of tea back in the refrigerator and pulled out a bowl of pitted cherries. "If you'd like to give it a try, I can lend you a chef's jacket."

The older woman smiled and took a sip of tea. "Another time, perhaps. Are you going to be able to save your dessert?"

"No problem." Picking up a knife, Mattie smoothed over a few rough spots in the frosting, then used the tube of parchment paper to even out J.D.'s "bullets." When she was satisfied, she began to poke the pitted cherries into the center of each chocolate lump. "What do you think?"

"Your guests will think you planned it that way." Lynda took another sip of tea before she set down the glass. "I'd like to be honest with you, Ms. Farrell. I didn't come here today just because of my daughter's phone call. I came to give you and Grant a little test."

Mattie gave her a level look. "Did we pass?"

"I don't blame you for being annoyed. My excuse is that I love my grandson. So I'm not going to apologize, but I would like to explain." At Mattie's nod, she continued. "I'm a rich woman, Ms. Farrell—"

"Mattie."

Lynda's lips curved. "Mattie. I inherited money and married more. I'm telling you this because my daughter is a lot like me. When you're rich, you think you can do what you want and get away with it. So far, my daughter has done just that. She married Grant and divorced him. Then she married again and took my grandson a continent away. Now, she's decided to give him back to his father, as if he were a bag of beans, because her new husband has decided that he wants her to devote all her attention to *his* son. I'd like to horsewhip the two of them." She shrugged elegantly. "In many ways, I'm just as spoiled and arrogant as my daughter. But I don't believe in divorce. I think it's a curse on the institution of marriage, and it destroys children."

Overhead, they heard the sound of running feet and laughter. For a moment, neither woman spoke. In the dining room, the harpsichord began to play a soft melody. A lullaby.

Lynda's gaze shifted to the doorway. "I'm fascinated by that harpsichord. It played earlier when the front door swung open." She turned back to Mattie. "I'd love to know how it works sometime, but for now, I'd appreciate it if you wouldn't repeat the sentiments I've just expressed about divorce to anyone. If the news got around, I'd be persona non grata at my country club."

"My lips are sealed," Mattie assured her with a smile. "And I can tell you that nothing is more important to Grant than J.D."

"I know his intentions are good. I just want to be sure that this change of life for J.D. is going to be permanent."

Mattie studied the woman sitting across from her. "I'm not sure why you're saying this to me instead of Grant."

Lynda laughed. "Oh, I've said it all to him several times. He knows exactly how I feel. I even considered suing for custody of J.D. myself. But I'm not sure that it would be the best thing for him." Resting her elbows on the counter, she leaned closer to Mattie. "I'm talking to you because I want to know what your intentions are toward Grant."

Mattie stared at the older woman. "What do you . . . ? Do you think that Grant and I . . . ?" Mattie lifted a hand and dropped it. "We're not . . . we're partners, that's all."

"Except that you love him."

Agitated, Mattie slid off her stool and began to pace. What could she say? The last thing she wanted to do was hurt Grant's chances of getting custody of his son. But she couldn't lie. She turned back to face Lynda Ackerman. "If you're asking will Grant and I get married? Will I be a mother to J.D.?" She raised her hands and dropped them. "I can't tell you." *Get married.* Even as she'd said the words, Mattie had felt a little skip of panic race down her spine. It wasn't what she wanted, was it? Grant had certainly never done or said anything to make her think . . . He wasn't even sure that he was going to stay in Barclayville. The only thing she was sure of was that Grant Whittaker loved his son. "If it's permanency you want for your grandson, you'll get it with Grant. I don't want you to worry about whether I might be a part of that."

"I appreciate your honesty, Mattie." Lynda barely finished her sentence when the harpsichord broke into a march, and Grant walked into the kitchen with J.D.

"The Clemson sisters just turned into the driveway," he said to Mattie.

"We'll go," Lynda said. Grant led the way, and at the door she turned back. "I almost forgot my other, and perhaps more legitimate excuse for dropping by." She fished a small scrapbook out of her purse and handed it to Mattie. "A friend of mine who runs an antique shop in New York gave this to me. Seems his father kept a pictorial history of the Barclay house in Manhattan. It's filled with newspaper clippings and magazine articles. He claims they moved all their furniture back home after they closed the mansion in Barclayville, so he thought we might be interested in looking through it. We can talk about it on Sunday if I'm still welcome."

"Of course you are," Mattie said.

Lynda was smiling as she turned to edge her way past Ada Mae and Lily in the doorway.

"Busy day?" Ada Mae inquired, looking around the kitchen.

"Extremely," Mattie said, glancing down at her clothes. "I have to change."

"Before you do that, we'd better get that dog out of the way." Ada Mae was halfway through the dining room, with Lily and Mattie at her heels. "He's blocking the front door."

And he was. The door was wide open, and Hannibal was a huge furry mound right in the center. It was the first time Mattie had actually seen him all the way up on the porch. But not one hair of him was actually in the foyer, she noticed as she edged her way past him. Then she saw it.

Hannibal had been sick. The mess he'd upchucked was on the lowest step where she'd put the biscotti and petit fours, not a crumb of which remained. Mattie turned back to Ada Mae and Lily. "He's sick."

"Hmmph. Serves him right, the garbage he eats," Ada Mae said. But she was already nudging the dog over and stroking his belly. "His heartbeat's fast, and his breathing's a little shallow."

Grant joined in the doorway. "What's up?"

"J.D. and I tried to wake Hannibal up by giving him some of the cookies and little cakes out of that basket George gave us. It seems to have disagreed with him." Mattie pointed to the mess as Grant stepped over the dog onto the porch.

"That's odd," he said. "He eats scraps all day long at the diner, and I've never seen him get sick before."

Ada Mae glanced up at him. "Dr. Stack will take a look at him. He's a good friend of George's."

It took all four of them to half carry, half drag Hannibal to the Toyota. Mattie removed the basket from the back seat to make more room for the dog.

Grant grabbed her arm. "Did you or J.D. eat any of this?"

"No. Why—" She broke off to stare at him.

"Who in the world would have given this kind of gourmet stuff to George?" Ada Mae asked.

"You don't think . . . ?" Mattie began.

"An anonymous gift from someone who doesn't know George very well. I don't know what to think, but I'm going to have Mac check it out."

9

"LONG LIFE TO HANNIBAL!" Lily raised her glass in a toast.

"Amen to that!" Ada Mae touched her flute of champagne first to Mattie's glass and then to her sister's.

It was at Ada Mae's insistence that they'd opened the champagne to celebrate the dog's recovery. Grant had called earlier to say that the vet had predicted Hannibal would be as good as new in twenty-four hours. But Ada Mae was celebrating a lot more than that. Once Mattie had told her what she and Grant had learned from George that morning, Ada Mae had looked happier than Mattie had ever seen her.

"What is this that we're looking at?" Ada Mae asked as she refilled her glass.

"It's a scrapbook," Mattie explained, setting it on the table. She'd brought it out in sheer desperation, hoping to divert the two ladies' attention. It was after midnight and they hadn't yet heard from Grant or Sheriff Delaney about the results of the lab tests on the contents of the gift basket. There was no way that any of them would rest until they found out whether or not someone had tried to poison George. Now that the guests had left, it was hard not to worry. "It's a pictorial history of the Barclay house in Manhattan. Grant's ex-mother-in-law gave it to me. An antique dealer who's a friend of hers gathered the pictures from newspapers and magazines. I'm supposed to look through it and get a feeling for the furniture so we can buy some authentic pieces for the mansion."

"Hmmph," was Ada Mae's only comment as she refilled all their glasses.

Lily stretched full length on the opposite sofa and spread out her caftan while Ada Mae began to page through the scrapbook.

"Some of the newspaper clippings have faded. How are we supposed to recognize an 'authentic piece' when we see one?" Ada Mae asked.

Lily raised herself on one elbow. "I can't see much of anything from here. The pictures are upside-down."

"If you didn't need a whole sofa, you could sit over here with us," Ada Mae told her, flipping over another page.

"Wait!" Lily set down her glass and pointed. "That's Amelia Barclay. Even upside down, I recognize her."

Mattie perched on the arm of the love seat and leaned closer to study the photograph. The picture was good enough to show that Peter Barclay's sister was a beautiful woman. Her dark hair was pulled back from her face and fell loose around her shoulders. She was standing next to an intricately carved desk.

"What was she like?" Mattie asked.

Lily lifted her champagne in a toast. "A fairy-tale princess."

Ada Mae snorted. "A wicked old witch."

"She was always nice to me," Lily said.

"Oh, she was always nice enough in public and on the surface. Sugar wouldn't melt in that woman's mouth as long as she was in front of a camera. But behind closed doors..." Ada Mae finished the rest of her champagne. "Some of the old servants could tell stories, I imagine."

"It seems odd to be looking at her the way she was so many years ago, when I'm going to be meeting her in person tomorrow," Mattie said.

"Amelia Barclay is coming to Barclayville?" Lily sat straight up on the couch. "What on earth for?"

"She wants to buy the Barclay mansion," Mattie explained.

Ada Mae frowned. "You're not thinking of selling, are you?"

"No, Grant is not going to sell the Barclay mansion. Her banker, Pete Desmond, asked us to meet with Miss Barclay, as a favor. She's very upset about the two skeletons being discovered, and he thought we might be able to set her mind at rest."

"She *should* be upset, if you ask me. They were found in her house!" Ada Mae refilled her own glass and Lily's.

Suddenly, Mattie remembered. "Ada Mae, did the Barclay family endow a scholarship at the Barclayville Elementary School?"

"In your dreams," Ada Mae said.

"Pete Desmond told us that he won a scholarship from the Barclays that allowed him to go to college," Mattie said.

Ada Mae frowned and shook her head. "He was adopted by the Desmonds when he was about a year old. A nephew is what they claimed he was. And they came into some money at the same time, enough to buy seventy-five acres from their neighbor."

When the phone rang, Mattie rose to answer it, then shook her head at the two women before she stepped into the foyer. "C.J., how are you?"

"Tired and fat," C.J. replied. "And sore. This baby is going to be a world-class soccer player. Did I wake you up?"

"No. The last guests left about a half hour ago."

"Listen, I only have a minute. Roarke took McBride for a midnight stroll, but he doesn't like to leave me alone for very long. My friend, Lieutenant Mendoza, has narrowed the license-plate numbers down to two down-state rental agencies. Now he's working on a list of people who rented a black limousine from them in the past two weeks. It'll probably take some time. Are you all right?"

"Fine," Mattie said.

"Uh-oh, Roarke's back. I'll call you when I know more." She hung up.

"My sister-in-law," Mattie explained to the two polite, inquiring glances. "What did I miss?"

Ada Mae upended the champagne bottle over her glass and hiccuped. "You missed out on most of the champagne."

"Here she is again," Lily said, angling the scrapbook so Mattie could get a better view. "She's standing right next to a portrait of her parents. And look at that armoire."

"Where's Peter Barclay?" Mattie asked.

"Dead," Ada Mae replied as she reached for Lily's glass.

Lily snatched it away from her sister and drained it before she set it back on the table. "He died before he could begin his second term as senator. Everyone said that Mattie Whittaker broke his heart, and he never recovered. It was so romantic."

Ada Mae made a noise halfway between a hiccup and a snort. "Romantic, my foot. I wouldn't be at all surprised if his sweet little sister did him in."

Mattie turned to Ada Mae. "You can't be serious."

Ada Mae pointed a not quite steady finger at the picture. "Follow the money trail. That's what they do on the detective shows. Who ended up with all the loot? She probably bricked up those two women, too." Ada Mae aimed her finger at Lily. "Why don't you ask your tarot cards about the money trail?"

Lily frowned at her sister and shook her head. "I am definitely driving home tonight."

Just then, the harpsichord began to play and the front door swung open.

"That's what I call a welcome," Mac Delaney said as he stepped into the foyer with Grant and Hannibal on his heels.

"What did you find out about the stuff in the gift basket?" Mattie asked.

"Rat poison," Grant said and leaned down to help Hannibal settle in front of the door. The dog made a sleepy noise deep in his throat.

"The technician at the lab said it would have taken more than half the basket to kill anyone," Mac told her, "but the staff at the hospital is very happy that George gave it to you. They're mounting their own special watch to protect him. And I've got a couple of state troopers who've volunteered to keep him under twenty-four-hour surveillance. Seems they like George's coffee."

"You think George is in danger?" Ada Mae rose a little unsteadily to her feet. Lily was almost as wobbly getting to hers.

"Not anymore," Mac said as he noted the empty champagne bottle. "It's just a precaution. I'm big on precautions, ladies. And that's why I'm going to give you a lift home and have someone deliver your car in the morning."

As soon as they left, Grant started to pace. "I told Mac everything we know or suspect, including what George told us about the night of my great-aunt's death. I offered to pay for a private detective to check dental records. And the state police are also going to swing by here as often as they can." He and Mac had gone over everything several times. But even now, saying it out loud, he was still restless. Moving to the small bar near the window, he found beer, twisted off the cap and took a long swallow.

He was tired, Mattie thought. And worried. "Did Mac find out anything about the license-plate numbers?"

Grant shook his head. "Nothing yet."

Mattie told him about C.J.'s phone call.

"I'll leave a message on Mac's machine."

"Give him Mendoza's name. If C.J. goes into labor, Mac can save us all some time by dealing directly with the lieutenant." While Grant punched numbers into the phone, she picked up the scrapbook. She was about to close it when she froze.

The woman in the portrait was wearing a locket. Mattie glanced at the caption. It read: Mrs. Peter Barclay, Senior, on the occasion of her son Peter's christening. Mattie lifted the book for a closer look at the locket—two interconnected hearts. Just like the one Hannibal had dug up in the fireplace.

"What is it?" Grant moved closer to the table.

Mattie explained briefly about the scrapbook, then she pointed to the locket. "Look, it's the same one that was found with the two skeletons. I'm sure of it."

Grant studied the picture. "It's similar."

"Just suppose that it's the same one." Mattie set the scrapbook down. "And suppose we were right in the first place, and the other skeleton in the fireplace belongs to Rachel Williams." Mattie turned to face Grant. "We've been assuming, at least I have, that Peter Barclay got a servant girl pregnant." Mattie waved a hand. "Secret trysts, whatever. She believed he was going to marry her, but he never intended to."

Mattie began to pace. "What if it wasn't just sex? What if Peter Barclay really fell in love with Rachel and gave her a locket that belonged to his mother? Then he gets called away to serve his country before they can marry. She told everyone that the father of her child was going to marry her. The Barclay family couldn't have been happy about it. By the time he returns, she's disappeared. Tragedy conveniently avoided. Then two years later, Peter Barclay falls in love with your great-aunt. True, she's not a servant, but she's not from their social sphere, either. So the whole problem starts all over again."

Rising, Mattie began to walk again. "We know how your great-aunt was lured up to the mansion. The same thing could have happened to Rachel Williams. Once the mansion was closed for the winter, there'd be no one there to witness a murder."

Grant went to her then. Her skin was like ice when he touched her. He ran his hands up and down her arms, then took her hands and led her to the couch. After settling her on one of the cushions, he sat beside her. "There's nothing you can do. Besides, aren't you forgetting the letter George received was from Rachel Williams?" Grant asked.

"Someone else could have written it, just as someone else wrote the letters that were supposedly from Mattie Whittaker after she died."

Grant's eyes narrowed. "You think Amelia Barclay had something to do with the deaths of those women?"

Mattie raised both of her hands. "Ada Mae said it tonight. 'Follow the money trail!' Amelia Barclay ended up with all the money. She wouldn't have if Peter had married and had children. And Lynda Ackerman said it this afternoon. A wealthy woman thinks she can get away with almost anything. Why not murder?"

"But George says Mattie's death was an accident. Amelia Barclay wasn't anywhere near her when she fell."

With a sigh, Mattie leaned back against the cushion of the couch and pressed her hands to her temples. "You're right. So much for my brilliant theory. We're right back to square one."

Grant took one of her hands and linked his fingers with hers. "It's perfectly possible that what's happened to us has nothing to do with the deaths of those two women." It was a possibility that he and Mac Delaney had discussed at length.

"Then why did someone try to feed rat poison to George?"

Grant leaned back against the cushion, too. "You've got me there."

For several moments, neither of them moved. They just sat together holding hands. The house was quiet, except for Hannibal's gentle snores. And the harpsichord. She didn't know when it had begun playing. The air still carried the lingering aroma of the meals she'd prepared, and there was the scent of lilacs, too. She was relaxed now, Mattie realized. She hadn't even understood how tense she'd been until now. For a second, she allowed herself to think that this was the way it might always be. Just a second, she promised herself. Then her stomach growled.

"You're hungry," Grant said. "Me, too."

When she looked at him, his eyes were closed. Her own eyes narrowed. "How about whipping up something to show me what a great short-order cook you are?"

He smiled, but he didn't open his eyes. "I believe that it states quite clearly in our partnership agreement that you have the final word on food."

Disengaging her hand, Mattie rose and gathered up the champagne glasses. She was in the archway to the foyer when she said, "And I say, let them eat cake."

Cake is what she brought back, along with tall glasses of milk. After two huge bites, Grant said, "You know, I would have been proud to serve this in George's Diner." He speared a lump of frosting on his fork. "Bullets stuffed with cherries. This is one time I fully approve of the presentation."

"And the taste?"

Grant shot her a grin. "I've never had a problem with your taste."

Hannibal whined, a long, low sound that started deep in his throat and finally exited through his nose. Mattie and Grant both turned to stare at him. The dog had opened his eyes and had roused himself enough to prop his head on his paws.

It was the most active that Mattie had seen him all day. "Is he all right?"

"He wants cake," Grant said.

"No way! The vet prescribed a light diet. I'll fix him an egg." She hurried out of the room.

While she was in the kitchen, the harpsichord began playing a familiar melody. It was the same tune that had been playing earlier, when she and Lynda Ackerman had been talking about J.D.

Grant was kneeling beside the dog when she returned to the front parlor with Hannibal's dish. He glanced up at her, and she paused.

"What's wrong?" Mattie asked.

"That music, what is it?"

Mattie listened for a moment, concentrating. "A lullaby. Brahms's 'Lullaby,' I think."

Grant rose and walked to the portrait. "She used to play it for me. I remembered the sound of the harpsichord the first night I came here. It was a different song, but I knew I'd heard that sound. Almost like a music box. I'd always thought that I'd dreamed it."

After setting the bowl down for Hannibal, Mattie slipped her hand into Grant's.

"I lived here until I was ten. My father hated her. He blamed her for everything. He used to say that we wouldn't be stuck in a dead-end town like Barclayville if she hadn't ruined everything." Grant shook his head. "I've always blamed her, too. But whenever I was sick—and other times, too—I'd hear that song." Grant turned to Mattie. "You're right, you know. She didn't put a curse on this town. Everything we did, we did to ourselves. But it was easier to blame Mattie Whittaker."

Mattie slipped her arms around Grant and rested her cheek against his chest. "You can't blame yourself for what you believed as a child. Maybe it helped you to survive. That's what she would have wanted." She looked up at him. "And now you're going to make a home for yourself and your son here. That's also what she wants."

"And what do you want?" Grant asked.

"My inn." It was the truth, and it was a lie. Standing there with her arms around him, she knew she wanted more. Drawing back, she hurried on. "Operating a country inn was my father's dream. He died before he could make it a reality. I'd like to think that he'd approve of what I'm doing here."

Grant didn't know what he'd expected. She'd always been up-front with him about her goal. She'd wanted to keep their relationship strictly business. Well, their relationship was personal now. And it was going to stay that way. He'd make that very clear to her as soon as he was sure she was safe.

"It's funny," Mattie mused aloud. "My father always thought it would be safe out here in the country. I wonder what he'd think of all this murder and mayhem?"

"Tell you what, let's forget it." He framed her face with his hands and brushed his lips across hers. If he couldn't tell her that he wanted her to be a permanent part of his life, he could show her. "Just for tonight."

Grant unfastened the buttons on her blouse, one by one, and took his lips on a journey down her throat, along her shoulder. The touch of a tongue, the nip of teeth. Mattie savored each and every sensation.

Always before, their lovemaking had been like a summer storm, brief but violent, breathtaking in its power. This time neither of them felt the need to rush.

He kissed her slowly, deeply, then changed the angle and began again. All the while, he was loosening her clothes, releasing the hook of her bra, the snap of her slacks. One by one, the pieces slid to the floor.

Mattie found even the brush of the material over her skin erotic, but it was his kisses that were clouding her mind. Her arms felt heavy, weighted, as she drew his T-shirt up over his head. There was no need to rip and tear. This time, she took delight in each new inch of skin she bared. She slowly drew his jeans down his legs.

She couldn't tell him yet that she loved him. Perhaps she never would. But she could show him with the brush of her fingers, the press of her palm. She could let him know with her mouth, which followed the same slow path her hands had taken. *I want you. I need you.*

Still without speaking, they moved to the love seat and lowered themselves onto it.

Naked, she lay on top of him. How strong her body was, how agile. How smooth her skin was, how soft. Again, he ran his hands over her shoulders, down her arms and up her sides to rest along the sides of her breasts. Everywhere he touched, he felt her heat. And the heat was for him.

He watched her face above his, spellbound by the way her breath would catch then rush out, the way the light slanted on her hair, highlighting first the red then the gold. So this was temptation.

Desire drifted around them, soft and dreamy, but no less strong than it had been before. Mattie felt the sensations move through her, just as intense, but this time she could treasure each one.

There was music. Not a lullaby now, but something with passion steadily building. Beethoven or Debussy? She couldn't clear her head enough to decide. Not with his scent wrapping around her. A hint of soap, and sunshine, and something else dark and mysteriously male. And his taste. Salty, tangy, and so potent. So this was seduction.

When he lifted her hips so that he could slip into her, it was as if they'd never been apart. There was no flash of heat, no explosion of need to sweep them away. And neither of them gave voice to what they were feeling. *You. Only you.* Together they moved slowly, determined to draw out the pleasure.

Her eyes were open, clouded but intent. He could see himself reflected there. Even when his blood began to pound, he kept the rhythm easy, patient, almost lazy. They had all the time in the world. There was a sweetness here they hadn't thought to find, a tenderness they hadn't thought they'd needed. Defenses dissolved, and they climbed on and on until ecstasy overtook them.

I love you.

The words, still not spoken, were pledged. Freely.

10

MATTIE PLACED the last goblet of triple-chocolate mousse in the refrigerator. The last thing she had wanted was a romance. But that was exactly what she was having.

Of course, it wasn't exactly a conventional romance. So far, there hadn't been any moonlight or candles. Just four new tires for her car because he cared about her safety. And he was a fan of her cherry-stuffed bullets.

More important, he was learning to accept her independence. Although he'd invited her to go with him to the diner this morning, he'd been understanding about her refusal. And he hadn't even called once to check on her.

With a damp cloth, Mattie swiped the rest of the mousse off her counter. The only little cloud hanging over their romance was the fact that she'd fallen in love with Grant Whittaker. And love had a way of making you want things that you just couldn't have. There was a knock on the back door and she whirled, her heart in her throat. She calmed down when she saw that the young man standing on the other side of the glass panel was wearing a uniform with a badge. He was holding up his identification. She hurried to open the door.

"Ma'am." He tipped his hat and slipped his ID into his pocket. "Sorry if I startled you. George Schuler's dog is blocking the porch steps. I didn't want to disturb him."

"It would take a bomb," Mattie said.

The young officer flashed her a grin. "He'll surprise you. A couple of times I've seen him get stirred up at the diner. My partner and I were just over there. Sheriff Delaney asked us to come by and relieve the car he sent earlier."

Mattie's eyebrows snapped together. "Delaney sent over a car?"

The officer nodded. "He told us about the trouble you're having and how you saved George from eating those doctored-up cookies."

"But I didn't—"

"We'll be parked in your driveway for a while. We didn't want you to worry." He waved a hand as he walked away.

Mattie closed the door and threw the dead bolt. No wonder Grant hadn't bothered to call her all morning. Hands on hips, she strode out of the kitchen, clearly imagining Mac and Grant huddled over the counter at the diner, hatching plots. Behind her back!

She sailed halfway through the dining room, then turned and marched up to the harpsichord. "I have a few things to say to that great-nephew of yours."

The harpsichord was silent.

"A partnership is a two-way street." She pressed a hand to her chest. "I'm not supposed to make a move without him. We're supposed to be working together. And right this minute he's at the diner with Mac Delaney discussing the case and making plans without me. I'm left out in the cold with the state troopers to protect me! And he finds himself a new partner. No way!"

Mattie began to pace. "Finding out what really happened to you and Rachel Williams was my idea." Pivoting at the entrance to the dining room, she tapped her foot. "*I'm* his partner, and he's stuck with me. There's no way I'm going to let him get away!"

There was total silence in the room. Not so much as a note from the harpsichord to distract Mattie as she replayed what she'd just said in her mind. Her hands were suddenly damp.

Wiping them on her jeans, she sank into the nearest chair. She'd meant every word, especially the part about not letting Grant get away.

She thought of Lynda Ackerman's question. What *were* her intentions toward Grant? She hadn't wanted to think about it then. She didn't want to think about it now.

She heard music. A glance at the keyboard told her that this time "Mendelssohn's Wedding March" was all in her head, but someone had gone to a great deal of trouble to plant it there. "You had this in mind all along."

There was no response to the accusation. Mattie stood up. "What does your great-nephew have in mind? That's the real question."

Silence again.

Mattie walked down the hallway to the foyer. The whole house was quiet. Too quiet. The door hadn't swung open for the state trooper. She glanced at the urn. It was beneath the banister where she'd shoved it the day before.

Mattie wandered into the front parlor. Sun splashed through the curtains, creating lacy patterns on the sofas and across the floor. There was a kind of hushed expectancy in the air, as if the house was waiting for something to happen.

Pete Desmond and Amelia Barclay were coming at two o'clock. Could the house be aware of that?

Premonition? Anticipation? *Nerves*, Mattie decided as her stomach growled. Then suddenly, the silence was shattered by the harpsichord. Mattie whirled, the door swung open and Grant stepped into the foyer.

He moved to her and pulled her close. For just a moment, he needed to hold her, kiss her, remind himself of her softness, her strength. When he was with her, it was easier to convince himself that he could keep her safe.

"Now, that's what I call a homecoming," Mac Delaney said as he followed Grant into the house.

When Mattie found the strength to pull back, she had trouble summoning up the annoyance she'd been feeling earlier. But she gave it her best shot. "You're late. I was just about to send the state troopers after you."

Grant smiled. "I was with the sheriff."

"I thought our deal was we'd work on this case together."

"I invited you to come with me to the diner this morning," Grant said as he led the way into the front parlor.

"While we're filling you in, I want to see the picture of the locket," Mac said.

Mattie picked up the scrapbook and began to flip through the pages. "We'll have to hurry. Pete Desmond and Amelia Barclay are due at two o'clock."

"I called Pete and invited them here for dinner, instead," Grant said. "After all, what better way to soothe Amelia's apprehension than to show her what we'll be trying to do with the Whittaker Inn?"

"And you didn't think you should call and let me know?" Mattie asked.

"We couldn't get through," Grant said. "We let it ring for a long time."

"That's funny," she said. "I didn't hear the phone ringing."

"I'll be here for dinner, too," Mac added, "so reserve a couple of tables. That way, I'll be free to hang around for the meeting. Did you find the picture yet?"

Mattie pointed to the locket. "The woman wearing it is Peter and Amelia's mother. The picture was painted when Peter was christened. Do you think Amelia had something to do with Mattie Whittaker's death?"

"My money's still on Pete," Grant said. "His name's on the limo lease."

"What?" Mattie almost dropped the scrapbook.

"I called your sister-in-law's friend, Lieutenant Mendoza, and asked him to pass along Amelia Barclay's and Pete Desmond's names to the people who were compiling the list of people who may have rented a black limo from the rental agencies. He called us back with a match just before we left the diner." Mac took the locket out of an envelope and held it next to the picture. "I don't think we should underestimate anyone who's already killed twice. I want to be there when you meet with them." Mac studied the picture. "It looks like the same locket, but the picture's awfully small. May I borrow it? Someone in the police lab can enlarge it."

Mattie handed him the scrapbook. "If Pete Desmond was alive at the time of Rachel Williams's death, he would have been a baby. And he couldn't have been much older when your great-aunt died. Besides, George didn't mention any kid on the scene."

She was interrupted by a sudden pounding on the front door. Mattie and Grant both jumped up and stared into the foyer.

"You look as though no one has ever knocked at your door before," Mac said, moving to answer it.

He opened the door to a young uniformed officer who nearly saluted. "Sheriff Delaney. We just got a call from our dispatcher. A Mrs. Ackerman is trying to get in touch with Grant Whittaker. Says it's an emergency and that the operator told her this line is out of order."

Grant reached the phone first. "Dead," he announced. "That's why we couldn't get through earlier." He took Mattie's hands. "I'll go to the diner and call from there. It's the closest place. I won't be gone long."

Grant was halfway across the lawn, out of earshot, when the officer turned back to Mac. "We've got to go, too," he said. "There's a fire at the Williams farm along County Route 35 near Tyler's Creek."

"What is it?" Mattie asked, coming up behind Mac.

"Fire at the old Williams place," Mac said.

The younger man added, "Neighbors claim they heard an explosion."

"Mattie," Mac said in a hesitant voice.

"Go," she said. "I'll be fine."

"Grant's going to be upset. But you'll be fine if you just stay here inside the house. Give me your word."

"Where am I going? I don't have a car."

When Mac's truck pulled out of the driveway, silence descended on the house. After throwing the dead bolt, Mattie glanced at her watch. Two o'clock. Her thoughts turned to tonight's menu. There was time, she supposed, to research the perfect potato dish, but a risotto would also go nicely with the veal and salmon entrées.

She wandered restlessly into the front parlor, and the glint of sunlight on gold caught her eye. Mac had left the jewelry lying on the table. Impulsively, Mattie reached for the engagement ring and slid it on her finger. It fit. She held up her hand and sent prisms of light dancing along the walls. Then she put the locket around her neck.

Some people thought that stones and metal could trap emotions. She tried hard to imagine what Mattie Whittaker must have felt when the man she loved gave her a ring as a pledge of his love. The joy flowed through her, deeper than she'd expected.

How would it have felt to have that love betrayed? Closing her eyes, Mattie concentrated. But she couldn't feel it. And that had been the problem all along.

The anger, the hurt, the grief. All the emotions she'd felt when her partner had betrayed her. Try as she might, she couldn't reconcile those emotions with the mischievous spirit who had played "Mendelssohn's Wedding March" every single time Grant Whittaker walked through the front door. The same spirit who had played him lullabies when he was a child in this house.

She looked up at the portrait and felt certain that Mattie Whittaker had not been deceived by her lover. And Rachel Williams? Closing her eyes, she wrapped her fingers around the locket and concentrated. There was a different feeling here. Sadness. And a longing. Would she be able to feel stronger vibrations at the mansion? Opening her eyes, she began to pace again. Did she dare go up there . . . ?

"Forget it!" she said aloud. She'd given her word to Grant and Mac. Then another thought occurred to her. Maybe if she could just look at the place . . . The third floor was visible from the window in her office. She hurried up the stairs.

The cold spot stopped her like a wall of ice. She stepped back, clutching the banister to keep her balance.

The harpsichord started to play for the first time all day. Slowly, Mattie walked downstairs and headed into the dining room.

The piece wasn't familiar, and as soon as the melody finished, it began again in a lower key. Mattie Whittaker was trying to tell her something. As she moved closer to the harpsichord, the tempo increased. She looked beneath the lid to watch the hammers hit the tightly strung wires, faster and faster as the melody built into a thundering crescendo.

When the music stopped, Mattie stared at the now-still wires, knowing exactly what had happened the night of Mattie Whittaker's death. Knowing how a woman could commit a murder, but appear to be totally innocent.

She had to tell Grant and Mac. Halfway to the kitchen, she remembered that the phone was dead. But then someone knocking on the back door kept her going. Maybe the state troopers were back.

It was Pete Desmond she saw through the glass, and he looked distraught. His hair, usually neat, was windblown, and beads of perspiration dripped down his face. Mattie opened the door.

"Please . . . the phone." His voice was raspy, breathless.

Mattie drew him into the kitchen and shoved him onto a stool. "My phone is dead," she told him, while searching for the brandy. She poured a generous amount into a glass.

"An ambulance," Pete managed to say before he took a swallow.

"I'll run to the diner and make the call from there as soon as I know what's going on," Mattie said.

He took another drink of the brandy, and his voice was stronger when he spoke. "I haven't run that fast in a long time. It's Miss Amelia. She was so angry when I told her our meeting with you was postponed. I've never seen her that way." Taking out a handkerchief, he mopped his forehead. "The only way I could calm her was to bring her to the mansion so that she could go through it and see how it's weathered the years. I thought everything would be fine. But she fell. On the stairs."

"Is she all right?"

"I'm not sure. I didn't want to move her. And she was afraid to be left alone. Told me to come here and phone for help."

"So she was talking?" Mattie asked.

Pete waved a hand. "Fading in and out. Look, could you go up there and stay with her while I get help?"

On her way out the door, Mattie grabbed the bottle of brandy.

GRANT PACED along the length of the counter in George's Diner. He glanced at his watch. A full half hour had passed since he'd spoken to Lynda Ackerman's butler, who was unaware of any emergency. According to Martin, J.D. and his grandmother had gone to a movie at one of Albany's malls.

It had seemed more efficient for the butler to track them down, so Grant was stuck waiting and twiddling his thumbs, trying not to think about how dangerous malls were for a kid. There were all those levels with railings to pitch over. And what better place to snatch a kid than at a mall?

Swearing, he ran his hands through his hair and made himself sit on one of the counter stools. Lynda was a good grandmother. She would take every precaution. He consoled himself by recalling J.D.'s complaint that his grandmother always took him to the ladies' room when they went out together.

He'd managed to sit still for three minutes—a lifetime—when the phone finally rang. It was his ex-mother-in-law.

"Grant? What is going on? Martin had us paged in the middle of the movie."

"Is J.D. all right?"

"He's got grease stains from the popcorn on his shirt. But other than that—"

"State troopers came to my door. They said that you'd been trying to reach me. Some kind of emergency."

"I never called," Lynda said. "Here, I'll put J.D. on."

"Dad?"

"J.D., you're all right?"

"We're missing the best part of the movie."

"Listen, you give your grandmother a big kiss, and hurry back to see the rest of it. I'll call you tonight." Grant hung up the phone. Why would anyone . . . ?

As he tore out the door, he prayed that Mac hadn't left Mattie alone.

THE SUN BEAT DOWN on them as Mattie and Pete Desmond approached the Barclay mansion. The heat had formed a haze over the valley, and the air was still, full of the drone of insects.

Pete's breath was rasping again. She slanted him a glance as they neared the porch steps. His color was better since he'd had the brandy.

The front door was open. He took Mattie's arm to lead her up the porch steps. The foyer was empty.

"She was right here when I left."

"Peter . . ." The hoarse voice drifted down from the second floor.

"We're coming." Pete hurried Mattie up the first two steps until she pulled free of his grasp.

"C'mon." He reached for her arm again.

"I'm not going up there. That's how she killed the others."

"What?" He stared at her.

"Peter . . . please." The voice was closer this time, more insistent. "I can't breathe."

Mattie backed down two steps. "Amelia Barclay killed Rachel Williams and Mattie Whittaker and bricked their bodies up in the fireplace."

Pete stared at her. "What are you talking about? Amelia Barclay is the kindest woman I know, and she needs help."

"If you help her, you'll be an accomplice."

When his hand clamped on her wrist, Mattie knew a moment of panic, but she remembered the brandy bottle and smashed it on the banister, bringing the jagged edge within an inch of his wrist. "She's going to kill me. If you're not her accomplice, she'll kill you, too. I'm not going up there."

"Yes, you are, my dear."

Mattie turned and fixed her gaze on the woman standing behind the railing that swept along the upper hall. Her hair was silver gray and perfectly coiffed. Her voice was strong and very calm.

"Thank you for fetching her, Peter."

"Miss Amelia—"

"You can go now." Amelia Barclay waved her hand in dismissal. "Miss Farrell and I have business to settle. I knew you would come." She smiled at Mattie. "The women who were in love with my brother always came here to the house."

Keep her talking. That was all Mattie could think of. "I'm not in love with your brother."

"None of them were. It was the money, the house. So I killed them. Come up here, and I'll show you how I did it."

"I know how you did it," Mattie said. "With wire. You strung it across the top of the stairs."

Amelia moved then, and even in the dimness of the foyer, Mattie saw light glint off the chrome of the small gun in her hand. "Come up here now," she said.

For a moment, Mattie felt her muscles go weak. Her stomach had turned to ice. There was a buzzing in her ears. She didn't want to put a name to what she was feeling. She had to think. Pete Desmond's grip hadn't loosened on her wrist. But he hadn't left yet, either. If she had any hope at all . . . Mattie put her foot on the first step. Pete moved with her. "How did you convince Rachel Williams to come up here?"

Amelia laughed, a hollow, mirthless sound. "I wrote her a letter from Peter. She was being difficult, you see. If Peter had ever learned that he had a son . . . Well, I couldn't let that happen. In the letter, I told Rachel that he wanted to meet with her in her old room where they'd had their little affair. And it was there in the same room where she'd seduced my brother that I told her Peter didn't want her. He just wanted his son. She cried, of course. But in the end, she gave me little Peter because she knew it would be best for him if he was raised as a Barclay. And then she ran out of the room. She was so distraught that she fell down the stairs. Just as you're going to do, Miss Farrell."

Mattie climbed a step. "What happened to the little boy?"

"I arranged for him to be adopted and raised on a farm near his mother's home. I saw to his education."

"You made sure that George Schuler told Mattie Whittaker about him, didn't you?" Mattie asked. "You tricked her into coming to this house and you showed her the locket that your brother had given to Rachel Williams."

"She didn't believe me. She said she knew my brother too well. That he would never have knowingly deserted Rachel or her son. She took the locket, and she was going to tell Peter all about it." Amelia smiled. "But she fell, too. Now, it's your turn, Miss Farrell. I don't want to shoot you, but I will if I must."

Don't panic. Don't run. Mattie chanted the words in her head as she began to slowly climb the stairs. She didn't dare take her eyes off the woman standing above her, not even to glance at her watch. How much time had gone by? she wondered. How long had it been since Grant had left for the diner? She was on the fifth step when she caught the scent of lilacs and noticed the cold. Her fingers were suddenly numb.

Amelia felt it, too. The hand holding the gun trembled slightly.

Mattie moistened her lips, praying that her voice would be steady. "You won't be able to hurt me. I'm wearing the ring and the locket, gifts from your brother to the two women he loved. And Mattie Whittaker is with me right now. Can't you feel her?"

"No." Amelia took a quick step back from the top of the stairs. "Give me the locket. It belongs to me."

Mattie climbed up two more steps. "Mattie Whittaker wouldn't let you have it the night you killed her. She won't let you have it now."

Mattie heard the steps on the porch, heard Grant call her name. Then everything seemed to happen at once. Afterward, no matter how many times she replayed the events in her mind, she was never sure of the exact sequence of the sensations that bombarded her. Even as Grant called her name again, she heard the explosion and saw the flare of light as the gun released its bullet. A quick, hard push sent her hip banging into the banister and the broken brandy bottle spinning into the air just as the sudden impact to her right shoulder had her whirling. Then she fell.

SHE COULDN'T DIE. The words screamed through Grant's head as he raced toward her. Another shot exploded in the stillness. Grant felt the burning flash of heat near his cheek, then heard the splinter of wood. He dropped to his knees next to Mattie, who had just rolled onto hers. He grabbed her shoulders. "She shot you."

Mattie glanced down at the blood, then raised the flattened locket. "No, she shot this. It must have swung to my shoulder when you pushed me."

"I didn't push you, Mattie. I was at the foot of the stairs watching when you fell."

Behind them, Mac Delaney and two state troopers tore into the foyer, guns raised.

"Don't shoot. She's disarmed." It was Pete Desmond who spoke. One of his arms was around Amelia Barclay. With his other hand, he gripped the gun by its muzzle.

GRANT WAS ANGRY with her. He had a right, Mattie supposed. She had broken her word. But there had been extenuating circumstances. She pulled the last small balloon out of the refrigerator and carefully dipped it into a pan of cooling chocolate, then set it on parchment paper to cool and glanced at her watch. Noon. Five more minutes and she'd decide whether or not to go down to the diner and have it out with Grant.

He'd left the Barclay mansion with Mac and the state troopers to take Pete Desmond and Amelia Barclay to the jail in Mason's Corners. And he hadn't come back. She'd waited up for him all night. He hadn't even called. It had been almost twenty-four hours.

She'd hurt him by breaking her word. But she hadn't meant to. If she could just explain . . . Besides, if she hadn't gone up to the mansion, they might never have been able to prove that Amelia Barclay was the killer.

And then where would they have been?

"Amazing," Gina Farrell said, hurrying forward from the archway to the kitchen. Mattie jumped, and Gina apologized, "I didn't mean to scare you." She hugged her daughter, then climbed onto a stool and set a little cooler on the counter. "You're absolutely incredible. I never would have thought to use balloons as molds. How do you come up with your ideas?"

"Sheer desperation," Mattie said reaching for the kettle.

"No tea," Gina said, pulling champagne and orange juice from the cooler. "I thought we'd have Mimosas instead, to celebrate."

"Celebrate?"

"You solved the mystery. Now you can have your country inn." Finding glasses, she poured champagne, then added a dollop of orange juice before handing one to Mattie. She lifted hers in a toast. "May all your dreams come true."

Mattie set her glass down. "How did you find out?"

"C.J. called me right after after Lieutenant Mendoza called her. She knew I wouldn't want to hear from anyone else that you'd been shot."

"It's just a scratch. The bullet hit the locket I was wearing, and I wasn't really in any danger. She was right there with me, protecting me."

"She?" Gina asked.

"Mattie Whittaker. My ghost." Mattie began to pace. "How can I explain it to you? I'm not even sure I can explain it to Grant." She poured out the whole story of the two women whose lives had ended so tragically in the Barclay mansion. Then she climbed up on the stool next to her mother and explained what had happened the day before. "Grant is so angry. He said I broke my word. I'm not even sure that I have a partner anymore. What am I going to do?"

"Men want to be able to protect the people they love." She took Mattie's hand. "That's what your father's dream was about, you know. He loved us, and he wanted to protect us. If it had been just him, he would have been perfectly happy running that tavern in the center of town."

"But I was perfectly safe," Mattie said.

Gina rested her hand on her daughter's cheek. "None of us really knows that. Look at those two women you found in the fireplace. Look at your father. We never really know what tomorrow will bring."

"I'm interrupting," Ada Mae announced from the kitchen doorway. "Sorry." She waved a hand. "The front door's swinging open, but Madame Whittaker seems to be on strike. No music to announce your callers."

Mattie looked at her mother. "*She's* mad at me, too."

"Not me," Ada Mae said. "I dropped by to say thank you."

"For what?" Mattie stared at Ada Mae, noticing for the first time the color in her cheeks.

"For not paying any attention to me when I tried to talk you out of your plans for the Barclay mansion. I just came from the diner. I thanked Grant, too. I was wrong. Nothing good came from keeping secrets all those years. That's it," she said. "End of speech. Lily's waiting for me in the car." She patted the basket she was carrying. "We're taking some blueberry buckle to George. If he'd just told me everything fifty years ago.... Well, I have some things to tell him now." She smiled at Mattie. "We may be the first couple to see if that fool marriage curse has been lifted." She glanced over her shoulder. "Unless you and Grant beat us down the aisle."

Mattie watched Ada Mae walk away. Beside her, Gina sipped champagne and held her tongue.

"I can't . . . I mean, I don't know how he feels. We're business partners. We've never talked about . . ." Mattie picked up her glass and drained it. "He didn't come back here last night. He isn't even speaking to me. Besides, I have to finish making tonight's dessert."

"I could never have made those dessert cups, but I can certainly whip up something to put in them that won't embarrass you."

Mattie stood up, saying nothing, and Gina continued, "You certainly weren't afraid to run up to the mansion yesterday and face that crazy old lady."

Mattie almost ran out of the room.

GRANT TOSSED A PINT of freshly washed blueberries into the food processor, twisted the lid and started the motor. On a count of five, he stopped the whirring machine. A soft breeze sent the curtains billowing into the kitchen at the back of the diner. The temperature had cooled overnight. His anger hadn't.

He didn't want to face Mattie until it had, until he was sure that he wouldn't shake her or, even worse, demand something that she wasn't ready to give.

He blended sugar into the shortening, then sifted in flour and mixed. The problem was his. She didn't need him. And watching her face down a killer on that staircase yesterday had made him realize how much he wanted her to need him.

"Grant."

His head jerked up and he saw her standing in the doorway to the kitchen. For a moment, his eyes were unguarded, and she saw the need. It gave her the courage to walk forward.

"What do you want?" he said, and the coolness of his tone stopped her.

Perhaps she'd been mistaken. Maybe it was only surprise she'd seen in his eyes. Or maybe she'd only seen what she wanted to see. She searched her mind for something to say, for what she'd planned on saying. Her gaze fell on the food processor. With a frown, she walked over to it. "You smash the berries," she accused. "You make the cake blue on purpose!"

Grant shrugged. "It's the diner mystique. Appearance, zero. Taste, a ten." Because he wanted to go to her, Grant made himself lean against the counter. She was dressed in her usual work clothes, white jeans and a shirt. She was even carrying her briefcase as if she'd come to discuss business. Fine. He had some business of his own to discuss. "Would you like coffee?"

"Sure. I'll get it." Setting her briefcase on the counter, she took down two mugs and filled them, then handed one to Grant.

"You were right about Pete Desmond," he said. "Amelia's story wasn't always coherent, but it seems the only thing he was guilty of was signing the lease for the limousine. Amelia Barclay was the one who drove it. The day she locked you in the cellar, she had it parked behind the old stables. She also cut your phone line yesterday and called the state police pretending to be Lynda. Mac thinks she started the fire at the Williams farm, too."

"Pete—he's Rachel Williams's son, isn't he?"

"According to Amelia, he is. They're trying to locate the birth certificate and adoption papers. Mac says that she probably won't be found competent to stand trial. Evidently, whatever slim grasp she had on sanity slipped away when she heard that the skeletons had been discovered. She thinks that her brother is still alive and that he's in love with you."

Mattie took a sip of her coffee and set it down. This wasn't what she'd come here to talk about. But the fear had settled icy and hard in her stomach. Somehow, it had been easier to face Amelia Barclay's gun.

Grant set down his coffee untasted. He wanted to touch her. His hands tingled with the need to feel the softness of her skin. He balled them into fists at his side. He wanted to make love to her. But he wanted more than that. Perhaps more than she could give. That was the fear that kept him standing where he was. Just as it had kept him away last night. If he had gone to her, words would have been spoken, promises asked for, and perhaps denied.

It was Mattie who finally broke the silence. "I didn't come here to talk about Amelia Barclay. I know you're angry with me. And I'm sorry. I can see that you believe I broke our partnership agreement." She raised a hand to prevent him from speaking. "Maybe I did. Technically. But I was safe. Mattie Whittaker was with me. She saved my life when she shoved me into the banister. You know that."

Grant drew in a deep breath, hoping it would calm him. It didn't. "What I know is that I saw the bullet leave the gun. I saw it hit you and spin you around. And I watched you fall down those stairs." He could still see it every time he closed his eyes. "I only agreed to involve you in a partnership because I thought I could protect you." His laugh was quick and mirthless.

Mattie suddenly realized he was angry at himself, not at her. And there was no need. "You're not responsible for what I did yesterday. *I* am! And I'll probably do things in the future that you won't like, either. If we're going to be partners, you're going to have to accept that."

For the first time since he'd looked up and seen her standing in the doorway, Grant felt some of his tension ease. "Are you saying that we have a future?"

Mattie took a deep breath. "Actually, that's why I came to see you." She unzipped her briefcase. "I just got the papers from my attorney. I know we shook hands, but we never actually signed the papers."

"I won't sign them," Grant said.

For a minute, Mattie simply stared at him. There wasn't a trace of a grin in his eyes.

"Not unless we renegotiate some of the terms." He pulled a paper out of his pocket. "I made a list."

Her hands weren't steady when she reached for the paper and read aloud, "Number one, our relationship will be personal as well as business. Number two, we will provide a secure home for J.D. Number three, we'll get married." The paper slipped from her hand and drifted to the floor. "You want to get married?"

The stunned look on her face might have given him pause if he hadn't seen something else in her eyes. Hope? Fear? Whatever it was, it looked so much like what he was feeling that he had to smile. "I know how much you like lists." He pulled another one from his pocket. "I wrote out all the reasons why we should get married. First, there's the future security of the inn to consider. You won't have to be afraid that I'll leave or try to buy you out, or vice versa. And second, there's J.D. to consider. My attorney called this morning to tell me that Lisa has signed the custody agreement. All I have to do is add my signature. But J.D. would feel more secure if we were married. Third, if we get married, it will certainly please my great-aunt Mattie. She hasn't been subtle about her wishes, playing the wedding march every time I walk through the door. And last but not least, marriage would be a good way to prove that the curse has been lifted. Not that either one of us believes in it."

She was still silent, staring at him. Grant crumpled the paper he was holding and let it join the first one on the floor. "And not one of those reasons matters a hoot." He took her hands in his. "I want to marry you because I love you, and the only reason you should say yes is that you love me, too."

He was only inches away, and Mattie discovered that looking into the barrel of a gun had been easier than looking into Grant Whittaker's eyes. "I do." She let out a breath then, and with it went all of her fears, all of her doubts. "I love you."

Grant tangled his hands in her hair. "I love you, Mattie Farrell. I love everything about you. Even your lists."

They moved together into the kiss, their lips just touching at first, in a pledge, a promise. But it took only seconds for their desire to heat, their passion to ignite.

Her mouth clung and demanded, her body yielded and aroused. She could make him dizzy, weak with a kiss alone. Had it only been a day since he'd tasted her?

Suddenly, there was no patience in either of them.

"I want—" She struggled with his buttons and tore them open.

"I need—" He yanked at her T-shirt and pulled it over her head. His hands found soft skin, and he pulled her with him to the floor. When she was at last beneath him, he raised his head and tried to clear it. There was something he wanted to say.

"Grant?" She reached for him.

"Forever, Mattie. Our marriage will be forever. I want to have the ceremony in our new inn as soon as it opens. I want orange blossoms, organ music . . . the works."

"I think we'll have to settle for lilacs and harpsichord music."

Grant laughed and rested his forehead against hers. "I suppose we will. But the lilacs will go better with the blue wedding cake."

They were both laughing as she drew his mouth back to hers. "Say it again," she demanded.

"I love you."

"Forever," she whispered.

Epilogue

"I THINK I made a very big mistake."

Grant glanced up from adding a log to the fire to see his wife place a tray of desserts on the already loaded buffet table. She was wearing a long fringed sweater with an ivory skirt that swirled around her ankles when she turned and walked toward him.

"Then we'll cancel the party. I'd much rather celebrate our first anniversary privately," he said as he took her hands.

Mattie laughed as she looked at him. "It's also the first anniversary of the Whittaker Inn. And you agreed that Thanksgiving weekend was the perfect time to invite all our friends to join in our celebration."

"I reluctantly agreed," Grant reminded her.

"Well, it's too late to cancel. We can hardly turn them away at the door." Mattie raised his hand to rub his knuckle along her cheek. "I'm fine. And so is little Georgina or Matthew." She spread the fingers of his other hand over her stomach.

Grant felt the little punch that never failed to send his heart into his throat. He'd known about the existence of his daughter or son for almost seven months now, and the joy only continued to grow.

As the harpsichord began to play, he drew Mattie closer and looked around the main parlor of the Barclay mansion. The shelves were lined with books, a Tiffany lamp glowed on an old oak desk, chintz sofas and comfortable-looking chairs were arranged in conversation groups on gleaming wooden floors and the buffet table held a feast, for the eyes as well as the stomach. Here and there throughout the room, Mattie had placed pots of chrysanthemums. But above the scent of flowers and the aroma of food, Grant smelled the fragrance of lilacs.

"Okay, I give up," he said. "Everything looks perfect to me. What's the big mistake? Are you afraid that the food looks better than it tastes?"

"Never," Mattie said. "The mistake is that I ever let you talk me into putting George's blueberry buckle on our menu. I'm developing a craving for it. I ate two pieces while I was loading that tray."

Grant chuckled. "That just means our son or daughter will be born with a taste for plain old-fashioned diner food."

"Consider yourself lucky, Grant," Roarke Farrell said as he entered the room close on the heels of his fifteen-month-old daughter. "With C.J., it was take-out Chinese. I used to have to keep the refrigerator stocked with it."

"No one seems to like pickles anymore," Gina said as she shifted a few trays to make room for the bowl of mulled cider that Lily was carrying. Then Gina lit the candles. "There, I think we're ready."

The words were barely spoken when chaos erupted. Mattie heard muffled barking first, then the doorbell rang and the harpsichord went into a crescendo. The French doors flew open and the two dogs, Hannibal and McBride, tumbled in, skidding across the slippery floor until they landed in a heap of fur just short of the buffet table.

J.D. raced in on their heels, followed by Ada Mae and George close behind.

"Dad!" J.D. bellowed as he ran to Grant's side. "George says the pond's frozen over. We should be able to skate on it by Sunday! Can we? Can we?"

"Maybe Monday. We have a wedding reception here on Sunday." Grant ran his hand over his son's hair.

"Not another one. Why do so many people have to get married?"

Grant smiled. "You'll understand someday."

J.D.'s pout lasted only a moment, then the urge to inspect the buffet table apparently proved too strong.

"There *have* been a lot of weddings," Mattie said. "Who would have thought that the Whittaker Inn would become such a popular place to get married?"

Behind her, the harpsichord played a few bars of the wedding march. "Of course." Mattie laughed. "She wants to take credit for that, too."

The doorbell rang again, and together she and Grant greeted each guest as they arrived.

George and Ada Mae were meeting guests at the door, Roarke was taking coats, C.J. and Lily were ushering new arrivals into the main parlor. Lynda Ackerman managed a quick wave before J.D. dragged her over to the window to point out the pond.

Gina came up beside Mattie. "What is that song your great-aunt is playing?" she asked. "I know it, but I just can't remember the title."

"'Waltzing Mathilda,'" Mattie whispered. "But don't encourage her. She's been playing it off and on ever since I got pregnant. It's her not-too-subtle way of dropping a hint."

"Lobbying is a more accurate description," Grant said.

"I've explained to her," Mattie continued, "that if the baby is a girl, she'll be Georgina after you and George. And a boy will be Matthew after his great-grandfather." Mattie shot a narrow-eyed look at the harpsichord. "But she hasn't given up."

"Why should she?" Grant asked with a grin. "She finally got to both of us with the wedding march. She thinks she'll wear us down this time, too." He winked at Gina. "My great-aunt wants another Mattie running around the house."

"Two Matties are more than enough," Mattie insisted.

Grant tilted her chin up and stole a quick kiss. "Don't worry, my love. Even if there were three Mattie Whittakers, I'd still choose you."

Above them, the girl in the portrait smiled.

Weddings by De Wilde

Since the turn of the century the elegant and fashionable De Wilde stores have helped brides around the world turn the fantasy of their "Special Day" into reality. But now the store and three generations of family are torn apart by the divorce of Grace and Jeffrey De Wilde. As family members face new challenges and loves—and a long-secret mystery—the lives of Grace and Jeffrey intermingle with store employees, friends and relatives in this fast-paced, glamorous, internationally set series. For weddings and romance, glamour and fun-filled entertainment, enter the world of De Wilde...

Twelve remarkable books, coming to you once a month, beginning in April 1996

Weddings by DeWilde begins with
Shattered Vows
by Jasmine Cresswell

Here's a preview!

"SPEND THE NIGHT with me, Lianne."

No softening lies, no beguiling promises, just the curt offer of a night of sex. She closed her eyes, shutting out temptation. She had never expected to feel this sort of relentless drive for sexual fulfillment, so she had no mechanisms in place for coping with it. "No." The one-word denial was all she could manage to articulate.

His grip on her arms tightened as if he might refuse to accept her answer. Shockingly, she wished for a split second that he would ignore her rejection and simply bundle her into the car and drive her straight to his flat, refusing to take no for an answer. All the pleasures of mindless sex, with none of the responsibility. For a couple of seconds he neither moved nor spoke. Then he released her, turning abruptly to open the door on the passenger side of his Jaguar. "I'll drive you home," he said, his voice hard and flat. "Get in."

The traffic was heavy, and the rain started again as an annoying drizzle that distorted depth perception and made driving difficult, but Lianne didn't fool herself that the silence inside the car was caused by the driving conditions. The air around them crackled and sparked with their thwarted desire. Her body was still on fire. Why didn't Gabe say something? she thought, feeling aggrieved.

Perhaps because he was finding it as difficult as she was to think of something appropriate to say. He was thirty years old, long past the stage of needing to bed a woman just so he could record another sexual conquest in his little black book. He'd spent five months dating Julia, which suggested he was a man who valued friendship as an element in his relationships with women. Since he didn't seem to like her very much, he was probably as embarrassed as she was by the stupid, inexplicable intensity of their physical response to each other.

"Maybe we should just set aside a weekend to have wild, uninterrupted sex," she said, thinking aloud. "Maybe that way we'd get whatever it is we feel for each other out of our systems and be able to move on with the rest of our lives."

His mouth quirked into a rueful smile. "Isn't that supposed to be my line?"

"Why? Because you're the man? Are you sexist enough to believe that women don't have sexual urges? I'm just as aware of what's going on between us as you are, Gabe. Am I supposed to pretend I haven't noticed that we practically ignite whenever we touch? And that we have nothing much in common except mutual lust—and a good friend we betrayed?"

Women throughout time have
lost their hearts to:

Starting in January 1996, Harlequin Temptation
will introduce you to five irresistible, sexy rogues.
Rogues who have carved out their place in history,
but whose true destinies lie in the arms of
contemporary women.

#569 *The Cowboy*, Kristine Rolofson
(January 1996)

#577 *The Pirate*, Kate Hoffmann
(March 1996)

#585 *The Outlaw*, JoAnn Ross
(May 1996)

#593 *The Knight*, Sandy Steen
(July 1996)

#601 *The Highwayman*, Madeline Harper
(September 1996)

Dangerous to love, impossible to resist!

RAC

MILLION DOLLAR SWEEPSTAKES

SWP-M96

THE WRONG BED

The Wrong Bed! The Wrong Man!
The Ultimate Disaster!

Christina Cavanaugh was *supposed* to be on her honeymoon. Except the wedding got temporarily canceled, their flight was delayed while the luggage went to Europe—and the bridal suite was flooded!

Hours later a frazzled, confused Christina crept into her fiancé's bed. But it was the wrong bed... containing the wrong man. And when she discovered the shocking truth it was too late!

Enjoy honeymoon bedlam and bliss in:

#587 HONEYMOON WITH A STRANGER
by Janice Kaiser

Available in May wherever Harlequin books are sold.

HARLEQUIN®

Temptation

BRIDE'S BAY RESORT

UNLOCK THE DOOR TO GREAT ROMANCE AT BRIDE'S BAY RESORT

Join Harlequin's new across-the-lines series, set in an exclusive hotel on an island off the coast of South Carolina.

Seven of your favorite authors will bring you exciting stories about fascinating heroes and heroines discovering love at Bride's Bay Resort.

Look for these fabulous stories coming to a store near you beginning in January 1996.

Harlequin American Romance #613 in January
Matchmaking Baby by Cathy Gillen Thacker

Harlequin Presents #1794 in February
Indiscretions by Robyn Donald

Harlequin Intrigue #362 in March
Love and Lies by Dawn Stewardson

Harlequin Romance #3404 in April
Make Believe Engagement by Day Leclaire

Harlequin Temptation #588 in May
Stranger in the Night by Roseanne Williams

Harlequin Superromance #695 in June
Married to a Stranger by Connie Bennett

Harlequin Historicals #324 in July
Dulcie's Gift by Ruth Langan

Visit Bride's Bay Resort each month wherever Harlequin books are sold.

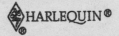

HARLEQUIN ®

BBAYG

Weddings by DeWilde

Since the turn of the century, the elegant and fashionable
DeWilde stores have helped brides around the world
turn the fantasy of their "Special Day" into reality. But
now the store and three generations of family are torn
apart by the separation of Grace and Jeffrey DeWilde.
Family members face new challenges and loves in this
fast-paced, glamorous, internationally set series. For
weddings and romance, glamour and fun-filled
entertainment, enter the world of DeWilde...

Watch for The RELUCTANT BRIDE by Janis Flores
Coming to you in May

Rita Shannon has just been hired as Grace DeWilde's
executive assistant. Helping to create the new
San Francisco store was a dream come true...until
Rita was forced to rely on deal-maker Erik Mulholland,
a man whose past betrayal still wounded her to the
depths of her soul.

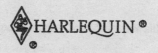

HARLEQUIN ®

WBD1

Fall in love all over again with

This Time... MARRIAGE

In this collection of original short stories, three brides get a unique chance for a return engagement!

- Being kidnapped from your bridal shower by a one-time love can really put a crimp in your wedding plans! *The Borrowed Bride*— by **Susan Wiggs**, *Romantic Times* Career Achievement Award-winning author.

- After fifteen years a couple reunites for the sake of their child—this time will it end in marriage? *The Forgotten Bride*—by **Janice Kaiser**.

- It's tough to make a good divorce stick—especially when you're thrown together with your ex in a magazine wedding shoot! *The Bygone Bride*— by **Muriel Jensen**.

Don't miss THIS TIME...MARRIAGE, available in April wherever Harlequin books are sold.

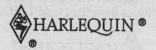

You're About to Become a *Privileged Woman*

Reap the rewards of fabulous free gifts and benefits with proofs-of-purchase from Harlequin and Silhouette books

Pages & Privileges™

It's our way of thanking you for buying our books at your favorite retail stores.

PROOF OF PURCHASE

HT-PP129

Offer expires October 31, 1996

Pages & Privileges™

Harlequin and Silhouette— the most privileged readers in the world!

For more information about Harlequin and Silhouette's PAGES & PRIVILEGES program call the Pages & Privileges Benefits Desk: 1-503-794-2499

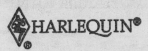

HARLEQUIN®

HT-PP129